BY: TIFFANY DOMENA

# PERCEPTION

THE WORLD'S MOST AFFLUENT LEADER

HOW TO CONNECT LOVE, POWER, AND PURPOSE TO TRANSCEND PERCEPTION

# PERCEPTION: THE WORLD'S MOST AFFLUENT LEADER
## CONNECT LOVE, POWER, AND PURPOSE TO TRANSCEND PERCEPTION

By: Tiffany Domena

Copyright © 2014 by Tiffany Domena.

http://www.mandatorysuccess.com

# TABLE OF CONTENTS

DEDICATION

7

ACKNOWLEDGMENTS

9

PREFACE

10

INTRODUCTION

13

CHAPTER ONE: GRASPING YOUR PURPOSE

20

CHAPTER TWO: BRACE YOURSELF FOR TRANSITION!

31

CHAPTER THREE: THE POWER OF LOVE

47

CHAPTER FOUR: THE POWER OF YOUR STORY

54

CHAPTER FIVE: THE BODY, YOUR TEMPORAL RESIDENCE

60

CHAPTER SIX: THE POWER OF IDEAS

75

CHAPTER SEVEN: THE POWER OF CREATION

91

CHAPTER EIGHT: THE POWER OF PROPERTY

96

CHAPTER NINE: THE POWER OF FAITH

103

CHAPTER TEN: THE POWER OF SUBMISSION

CHAPTER ELEVEN: THE POWER OF FORGIVENESS

CHAPTER TWELVE: THE POWER OF DILIGENCE

CHAPTER THIRTEEN: THE POWER OF VOLUME

CHAPTER FOURTEEN: THE POWER OF THE WORD

CHAPTER FIFTEEN: THE POWER OF THE BLOOD

ABOUT THE AUTHOR

OTHER BOOKS BY THIS

AUTHOR

OTHER PRODUCTS BY THE AUTHOR

AUTHOR

# DEDICATION

This book is dedicated to our readers, our family and friends in the present, and those to come in the future. May God always be the Crown Holder in your lives.

# ACKNOWLEDGMENTS

First and foremost, I want to acknowledge Love Himself, who renders all revelation, who inspired me to write this book, and who placed an outstanding husband in my life to encourage me to pursue my passion.

Secondly, I want to thank my firstborn son, Jaelin Richmond for giving me the time and encouragement that I needed to write, study, and correlate ideas. We love you!

Thirdly, I want to thank my team, my friend and sister, Tiffany Kelly for pouring so many great ideas, my Dad for always being open to sharpen and offer tons of wisdom, and my editors for working on this project with me.

Lastly, I want to thank all of my family and friends who encouraged me to put the pen on the paper, and allow God to speak thru me. May God bless you all!

# PREFACE

Health.com says. "Depression is more common than AIDS, cancer, and diabetes combined, and nearly 400,000 people attempt suicide in the U.S. every year." The U.S. alone houses nearly half a million people that desire to take their lives; even without adding the remainder of the world, this number is entirely too high. You were placed on this Earth for a reason!

The statistics of how many people do not know why they exist, what they are capable of doing, and why is astonishing. This book is intended to teach you to turn your heartache into laughter, your pain into prosperity, and a bad situation into leverage for astounding outcomes. Here, we will be providing a holistic, entirely natural medication for depression and suicidal ideation, and the power is all within you.

You have been created with all of the power required to transform any situation. The unfortunate thing is that you may not be receptive of your own embedded powers.

You are not alone. Dr. Myles Munroe says that most people use less than 10% of their potential.

If they do not understand their potential, or their reason for being alive, how can they appreciate it, and maximize their time? It's not possible.

Do you know what happens when a person lives their entire life without knowing *why*? Henry Thoreau says "they die with the song still in them", and Les Brown says, that the grave will become wealthier. Do not let this person be you! Live your maximum potential now! Begin today!

When your eyes are open to your power, you can maximize the use of them to fulfill your purpose. Have you experienced bad things in your past? Do you feel that you do not have skills? Do you experience depression or thoughts of suicide? Do you have desires on the backburner? If you can answer, "yes" to any of these questions, this book will definitely have revelation for you.

-If you are confused about your purpose or how to identify it
-If you know someone else that is dealing with an unsettled view of life
-If you are ambitious and moving towards your purpose, but need a little encouragement and transformational insight

Whether you are the smallest, slowest, poorest,

least knowledgeable, quietest, least-skilled, weakest, or whatever you consider your disadvantage, you have been implanted with the powers to be advantaged, and this book will show you how. If the ant can be at an advantage, so can you.

This book will offer you:

-Knowledge from the ant on love, power, and purpose
-Insight on your embedded powers
-Exercises for you to connect to your purpose
-Wisdom to help you identify and break self-hindering beliefs
-An opportunity to transform your environment and reshape it with others desiring to live a life led after love, power, and purpose

# INTRODUCTION

I sat in the library in distress. My computer had crashed and on it, I had stored my first book, Someone Covets You. I had uploaded the proof for review, but after doing so, I had noticed an error in the proof. I sat at the library computer distressed thinking, "I want to fix the minor defect with this book, but what will I do without my original document? Will I have to a retype all of this??!?"

As I was sitting pondering the resolution for my book, I was greeted by the gentlemen that sat next to me on the computer. He said, "How are you?". I said, "I am doing well, and you?".
He began this script that I had heard many times before. It goes something like this:

"Are you making the Air Force a career?" the person usually says.

"No". I reply promptly.

"The Air Force is the stable route", they say, then they discuss the experiences that they have had in the military; usually making light of the favorable and the unfavorable. I have no problem with the truly purpose driven military people (they do exist), but in this case, there was a level of inner dishonesty, a self-betrayal that was only recognized in the conversation.

It was beautiful to see that after I replied, "I believe that God wants to do something else with my life that the military cannot support," then he began to ponder and look within. He said, "Before I joined the Air Force, I was a saxophonist. I used to go on tour all over the nation to play my saxophone, and I loved it. When I joined the Air Force, out of basic training, I was placed in a small dorm room for technical training. I had a roommate that worked the opposite shift, so I did not want to disrupt his sleep by practicing the saxophone. Days became years, years became decades. I put my saxophone in storage years ago, and have not pulled it out."

I pondered his words; looking internally myself. Deciding to myself, "In 20-30 years, when the Air Force considers me retirement age, is this what I want to ponder?". He continued:

"I lost my first love. Since I have been in the Air Force, I lost my love of playing music, and I have lost my marriage."

"I responded, "It's not too late. The choice is still yours. What will it be?"

He said, "I'm gonna go get my saxophone out"

I said, "You promise?"

He said, "Yea. I am a man of my word, and I'm gonna do it."

This conversation resulted in an AMAZING revelation between the two of us. We discussed military career, talents, family, and many other topics all to resolve that "stability is vanity, and can be a huge sacrifice of your joy". At the close of the conversation, we both felt enlightened. We left with agreements: I would continue writing and painting, he would begin playing his saxophone again.

It was a defining moment in my life. Until then, I had not recognized the betrayal of my spirit that I could experience if I did not make the decision to separate from the military. As a result of this conversation, no longer did I say, "I want to do it", but "I have to do it", and I began planning my exit from the Air Force with defined parameters. God and I had committed to our success in making transformation in the world, and it was a really good, secure feeling.

The Bible says, "Go to the ant, you sluggard; consider her ways and be wise!—"(Proverbs 6:6). In my journey towards purpose, I began making small observations of the ant to ensure that I was properly grounding my choices.

Before beginning my journey towards purpose, I had only mildly pondered the wisdom of the ant in my annual journey of reading thru the Bible, but I did not extrapolate the topic in anyway similar to what I have done with this book. I'd heard of wisdom in their gathering, and I had some frictional memories of ants as pests.

I remember as a child, seeing large black ants swarming around spills of food items that were sweet. Then when I moved to Texas, I had a different experience with ants, they were no longer invaders of the indoors, but they were stinging conquerors of my exterior landscape.

I can recall several instances where I would innocently be enjoying the outdoors; basking in the wind, walking barefooted, enjoying the astonishing array of creation. When abruptly and without apparent warning, I would begin to feel an intense itch. Then, I would notice areas of my body with dermatitis; usually my legs or feet, but I have had instances where they would get areas that the sun does not shine for their feed. When I would touch the area of dermatitis, I found that it was several small raised bumps that were warm to the touch. From my recollection, I had not rendered any positive experience from ants. I would typically pay an exterminator to rid my property of their presence, and go on happily with my life.

However, in compiling the answers for this book, I found that God had poured a message into me of a perception of honor in the ants, and it seemed to wield a potentially destiny-unleashing consequence if I would conduct my focus as they do. It was VITAL for me to transform my perception of the ant from a pest to a receptacle of wisdom, begin to observe them, and allow their perspectives to transform mine.

In this book, each chapter contains a very brief observation of the ant, so that you can glean from their perspective to transform your own. The command to "look" is typically thought to be performed by the eyes. In this book, I will also be using this command to request that you tune to the Spirit. I will request that you look within, and be determined to see things from a new perspective than you see them now, and NEVER revert.

At the end of each chapter, I have exercises for you to complete. Each exercise is a part of the journey of transformation to love, power, and purpose. I want you to be transformed from a perception of fear to a perception of love. Remember, size is a perception; God grants human value, but all other values are assigned by you. This book will help you to stabilize your perceptions to something unchanging; love, power, and purpose. If you receive my request and respond to it in faith, you will be transformed from aspirations in the physical to aspirations in the spiritual, and when you have completed all of the exercises, you will have the tools to experience a fulfilling life; one that is pleasing to your Creator, and a life of love, power, and purpose.

## BEFORE VS. AFTER

| Before | After |
| --- | --- |
| Founds goals on temporal things | Founds goals on eternal things |

| Pursues things that stimulates ego or emotions | Pursues things that stimulate their purpose or the will of their Source |
|---|---|
| Works for temporal gain only: to pay bills, to supply immediate needs | Works for eternal gain (also supplies temporal needs): Making large positive impact on others, to train wise children, to leave a longstanding legacy that empowers |
| Gains direction from emotions, the perceptions and values of others, their senses | Gains direction from God, His Word, and wise counsel |
| Poor relationship quality | Great relationship quality |
| Poor money mentality: scarcity, compulsiveness, etc. | Wealthy mentality Ability to mute emotions, feelings, senses, and receive advice from God and wise people around them |

## REACH YOUR HIGHEST POTENTIAL!

| Abrupt in decision making: focuses on things that meet immediate needs | Attentive to times and seasons: Stores, harvests, an reaps in preparation for life's journey |

**THE WORLD NEEDS THE GIFT THAT ONLY YOU HAS!**

# CHAPTER ONE: GRASPING YOUR PURPOSE

"Your purpose is unique"

Many people live every day without knowing why. So little is spoken about why that majority of the world's populace acts on projected values that almost entirely create their perceptions, and thus perception has become the governing authority for most people in their daily lives.

Perception is the way that you view things. Perception encompasses worldview, religion, life experiences, beliefs, attitudes, feelings, ego, spirituality, and more. The unfortunate fact is that perception is not absolute; it differs amongst each individual, so what happens if you make your decisions solely based on your perception? What happens if my neighbor fails at entrepreneurship, and therefore perceives that it is hard and nearly impossible in today's economy, and I want to pursue it, and feel that it is possible? Is one of us wrong? In response to this question, Henry Ford said, "The man who thinks he can and the man who thinks he can't are both right. Which one are you?"

## REACH YOUR HIGHEST POTENTIAL!

The Bible says:

Plans fail for lack of counsel, but with many advisers they succeed. (Proverbs 15:22)

The plans of the mind *and* orderly thinking belong to man, but from the Lord comes the [wise] answer of the tongue. All the ways of a man are pure in his own eyes, but the Lord weighs the spirits (the thoughts and intents of the heart). Roll your works upon the Lord [commit and trust them wholly to Him; He will cause your thoughts to become agreeable to His will, and] so shall your plans be established *and* succeed. The Lord has made everything [to accommodate itself and contribute] to its own end *and* His own purpose—even the wicked [are fitted for their role] for the day of calamity *and* evil. (Proverbs 16:1-4)

Many plans are in a man's mind, but it is the Lord's purpose for him that will stand. (Proverbs 19:21)

For who [limited to human wisdom] knows what is good for man in his life, all the days of his vain life which he spends as a shadow [going through the motions but accomplishing nothing]? For who can tell a man what will happen [to his work, his treasure, his plans] under the sun after he is gone? (Ecclesiastes 6:12)

Tiffany Domena

## THE WORLD NEEDS THE GIFT THAT ONLY YOU HAS!

 Many times, we depend on our own perceptions to guide us, and forget that we are not the manufacturer of our lives. Just as each man-made product is created for a purpose and reason, so also are we.

In my book, Someone Covets You, I tell the story of a very seductive woman. She dresses provokingly, and her goal is to entice. She tells you everything that you like to hear. In her words, she says, "I play the lobes of their brains like the strings on a harp; making them feel, see, and hear their innermost desires." The catch to allying with her is that she has an underlying eternally detrimental mission. Her name is Sin and her husband is Death, and their ultimate goal is to keep you in their stagnated state of unproductivity and scarcity.

Many perceptions are infiltrated by Sin. Many people label sin religiously as right and wrong, and categorize it by the deeds of a person. Remember, we are spiritual beings having a human experience. Therefore, the heart is the ultimate measuring stick of Sin. Sin is succumbing to the externally established limitations. Again, Proverbs 16:2 says:

All the ways of a man are pure in his own eyes,

but the Lord weighs the spirits (the thoughts and intents of the heart).

As Dr. Myles Munroe said in his book, *Understanding Your Potential*, "Knowledge of man is learned, but the knowledge of God is discerned." You cannot submit entirely to the external knowledge, but seek God, and He will open His storehouse of abundant wisdom, and break every wall. How many times have you limited the manifestation of something God assuredly could have used you to do because of doubt? Jesus empowered us commanding us to overcome doubt in the story of Matthew 18, which says:

In the early dawn the next morning, as He was coming back to the city, He was hungry. And as He saw one single leafy fig tree above the roadside, He went to it but He found nothing but leaves on it [seeing that in the fig tree the fruit appears at the same time as the leaves]. And He said to it, never again shall fruit grow on you! And the fig tree withered up at once. When the disciples saw it, they marveled greatly and asked, how is it that the fig tree has withered away all at once? And Jesus answered them, Truly I say to you, if you have faith (a firm relying trust) and do not doubt, you will not only do what has been done to the fig tree, but

**THE WORLD NEEDS THE GIFT THAT ONLY YOU HAS!**

even if you say to this mountain, Be taken up and cast into the sea, it will be done. And whatever you ask for in prayer, having faith *and* [really] believing, you will receive.
And again, James warns us against doubt when he says, "Only it must be in faith that he asks with no wavering (no hesitating, no **doubt**ing). For the one who wavers (hesitates, **doubt**s) is like the billowing surge out at sea that is blown hither *and* thither and tossed by the wind." (James 1:6)

How many times has your perception been infiltrated by fear? Maybe you fear that someone has the credentials, following, or authority to succeed in your calling. Regardless of your background, size, shape, color, number of followers, or authority in your niche, you have been implanted with success. Your assignment is your assignment! Your purpose is as unique as the bevels on the tips of your fingers, and as the birthmarks that God uniquely bestowed on you.

Proverbs 6:6 says, "Go to the ant, you sluggard; consider her ways and be wise!—". The ant grooms their eggs within their colony. Before they have ever left, they have their roles, and they do not change. A leaf cutter ant will be groomed from its hatch from the eggs until he is mature enough to handle his duty as

## REACH YOUR HIGHEST POTENTIAL!

a leaf cutter ant.

The same is true with you. If God instilled the wisdom into the ants to assign a purpose, how much more do you think He has assigned a purpose to the one who was created in His likeness? He sent you here with an assignment. From your colony (heaven), He analyzed what the Earth needed, and assigned a spirit (you) to make the integral transformation in the Earth.

In Matthew 25:14-30, Jesus tells the outcome of those who do not unleash the potential that God has entrusted in you. He said:

For it is like a man who was about to take a long journey, and he called his servants together and entrusted them with his property. To one he gave five talents [probably about $5,000], to another two, to another one—to each in proportion to his own personal ability. Then he departed *and* left the country. He who had received the five talents went at once and traded with them, and he gained five talents more. And likewise he who had received the two talents—he also gained two talents more. But he who had received the one talent went and dug a hole in the ground and hid his master's money. Now after a long time the master of those servants returned and settled accounts with them. And he who had

## THE WORLD NEEDS THE GIFT THAT ONLY YOU HAS!

received the five talents came and brought him five more, saying, Master, you entrusted to me five talents; see, here I have gained five talents more. His master said to him, Well done, you upright (honorable, admirable) and faithful servant! You have been faithful *and* trustworthy over a little; I will put you in charge of much. Enter into *and* share the joy (the delight, the blessedness) which your master enjoys. And he also who had the two talents came forward, saying, Master, you entrusted two talents to me; here I have gained two talents more. His master said to him, Well done, you upright (honorable, admirable) and faithful servant! You have been faithful *and* trustworthy over a little; I will put you in charge of much. Enter into *and* share the joy (the delight, the blessedness) which your master enjoys. He who had received one talent also came forward, saying, Master, I knew you to be a harsh *and* hard man, reaping where you did not sow, and gathering where you had not winnowed [the grain]. So I was afraid, and I went and hid your talent in the ground. Here you have what is your own. But his master answered him, You wicked *and* lazy *and* idle servant! Did you indeed know that I reap where I have not sowed and gather [grain] where I have not winnowed? Then you should have invested my money with the bankers, and at my coming I would have received what was my own with interest. So take the talent

## REACH YOUR HIGHEST POTENTIAL!

away from him and give it to the one who has the ten talents. For to everyone who has will more be given, and he will be furnished richly so that he will have an abundance; but from the one who does not have, even what he does have will be taken away. And throw the good-for-nothing servant into the outer darkness; there will be weeping and grinding of teeth.

Do not bury what God has given you! You may be saying, "Okay. Okay. Where do I start? What do I have?". Moses asked the same thing when he was standing near the burning bush. There, as he journeyed alone, God had appointed him to free a nation. He said, "But behold, they will not believe me or listen to *and* obey my voice; for they will say, The Lord has not appeared to you."(Exodus 4:1) He outpoured with excuses that suppressed his desire to pursue God. Think about it, the nation of Israel was millions of people. He was raised in the palace of Egyptians who had been mistreating the Israelites for generations. He was being placed in the position of a traitor, and he was turning on the people that he called, "family": his mom (Pharoah's daughter), dad (Pharoah), and brother (Rameses).

Despite what he thought were deficiencies that inhibited his success, God wanted to use him. In ad-

## THE WORLD NEEDS THE GIFT THAT ONLY YOU HAS!

dition to turning on his family, Moses confessed to having speaking deficiencies. A man that led 3 million+ people having speaking deficiencies? How can that work? In our orderly thinking, manly minds, that would not work. He may need a speech coach or a branding coach, so that he can formulate his brand, right? Instead, God said, I am using you. He says the same thing to you today! His response to Moses was, "What do you have in your hand?", and my response to you is the same:

"What do you have in your hand?"

I will give you some clues, but the ultimate deciding factor will be rendered to you in your time of stillness. In the time when you escalate yourself beyond your thoughts; when you mute your senses and all other external input to your spirit, this will be the time when God can genuinely speak to you and you can discern your direction

-Free your talents and your story
-Examine your areas of mastery
-Examine your passions
-Examine your areas of increased wisdom
-Examine your connections

**REACH YOUR HIGHEST POTENTIAL!**

# PERCEPTION EXERCISE

### Required Materials:

- [ ] *Magazines that you enjoy*
- [ ] *Copies of Your best pictures (family and friends are welcome)*
- [ ] *Pictures of those that you admire*
- [ ] *Symbols of your desired mental, emotional, spiritual, and -economic status*
- [ ] *Any other symbols of things that you desire to manifest (ensure that these things are for the benefit of you and others)*
- [ ] *A board (any kind) sizeable enough to fit your images*

### Directions:

1. Go thru your magazines and cut out all of the images that are inspiring to you; images that make you say, "Wow. I wish I could do that".

2. Cut images out of the copies of your best pictures.

3. Cut out the pictures of those that you admire.

4. Cut out the symbols of your desired mental, emo-

**THE WORLD NEEDS THE GIFT THAT ONLY YOU HAS!**

tional, spiritual, and economic status.

5. Cut out all other symbols that you brought.

6. Glue them on your board to your liking.

7. Hang the board up in a place that you can see it several times daily.

**REACH YOUR HIGHEST POTENTIAL!**

# CHAPTER TWO: BRACE YOURSELF FOR TRANSITION!

In situations where you feel discontentment or perceive that something may be a threat to what you are attempting to execute, it is up to you to be aware of the present circumstance, perceive the threat, and to execute a solution. Life directed to purpose demands transition, so when you notice discontentment, here are some things that you need to do.

1. Acknowledge The Circumstance

Many times in the midst of your sign to move, you attempt to reshape your views towards the source. Sometimes you try to exercise tolerance. You find yourself arguing back and forth from the depths of your being because you are trying to project the dogma of the environment onto your life and destiny. I want to tell you, "Don't do that! Appreciate the individual that God made you!"

On many occasions, I can recall attempting to talk myself out of the feeling of discontentment. I say

**THE WORLD NEEDS THE GIFT THAT ONLY YOU HAS!**

things to myself like, "Tiffany, it is just XXX…. it's not that hard. You can do it", or, "Everyone else is doing this fine without complaining", or "Why don't I get it together?". Meanwhile, I am feeling the utmost discontentment about every element of what I am doing. Henry Miller said, "Life moves on, whether we act as cowards or heroes. Life has no other discipline to impose, if we would but realize it, than to accept life unquestioningly. Everything we shut our eyes to, everything we run away from, everything we deny, denigrate or despise, serves to defeat us in the end. What seems nasty, painful, evil, can become a source of beauty, joy, and strength, if faced with an open mind. Every moment is a golden one for him who has the vision to recognize it as such"

Going back to the wisdom of the ants, I noticed that when they were faced with fire, they all dispersed. Even when the flames moved very fast, and disrupted their communication signals, they instantly responded in flight.

You need to recognize the source of your discontentment, and then realize that your feeling of discontentment is the warning light telling you that it is time for a transition. If you feel this, a shift needs to take place. The shift will be coherent with God's

## REACH YOUR HIGHEST POTENTIAL!

Word, but will only take place by your command if you ask. Ignoring discontentment grows complacency. Be appreciative for the abrupt situation and your feeling of discontentment because thru it, the manifestation of your destiny is accelerated.

2. Take Your Thoughts Captive

The National Science Foundation says that humans produce as many as 50,000 thoughts per day. Throughout the day, most people are living life as if they are victims of their thoughts rather than taking them captive in the realization that their thoughts are their dominion. Your environment is a constant proponent of your thoughts. As you submit yourself to the observations of your senses (without putting these notions into biblical perspectives and grounding them in truth), you are allowing a fleeting perception to become your leader. In *My Stroke Of Insight*, neurosurgeon, Dr Jill Bolte Taylor said, "Unfortunately, as a society, we do not teach our children that they need to *tend carefully the garden of their minds*. Without structure, censorship, or discipline, our thoughts run rampant on automatic. Because we have not learned how to more carefully manage what goes on inside our brains, we remain vulnerable to not only what other people think about us, but also

**THE WORLD NEEDS THE GIFT THAT ONLY YOU HAS!**

to advertising and/or political manipulation."

Thoughts are infused by every sensory receptacle: hearing, sight, touch, taste, smell, our proprioception, and our vestibular. Many people allow their senses to control their thoughts and their imagination is being tainted on autopilot. Without the level of self-control- the discipline of taking time to address our thoughts- our lives are controlled by personal perceptions, and we grow further in separation from understanding and wisdom. Darren Hardy said, ""And as long as you're making choices unconsciously, you can't consciously choose to change that ineffective behavior and turn it into productive habits."

Inattentively, you begin saying to yourself things like, "I can't believe this is happening", "Who would have", or "How would they" in the midst of the signs for transition. When your thoughts are wandering on victim mode, you have stagnated the future from manifesting.

With the ants, little time was taken to focus on thoughts projected by perception. When you watch them respond to incidents, they do so without delay. In fire, the ants flee. In storms, the ants clinch together. When one dies, they continue

## REACH YOUR HIGHEST POTENTIAL!

moving towards their purpose undefeated. The ants are purpose-driven.

Emotional or sensory thoughts such as "this makes me feel", or "look how bad this looks", are distractions from the execution of your future. When you are too attentive to your physical perception, you lose sight of the spiritual truth of your purpose. In *The Compound Effect*, Darren Hardy said, "You get in life what you create. Expectation drives the creative process. What do you expect? You expect whatever it is you're thinking about. Your thought process, the conversation in your head, is at the base of the results you create in life," and in *The Secret* by Rhonda Byrne, she says, "thoughts become things". Making something sovereign (even thoughts) besides God is idolatry.

Idolatry is the fixation on the physical illusion rather than the connection with the Spirit of Truth. The Bible tells of stories of people who would create an idol of precious metals for worship. With this idol, they would submit themselves to it in prayer, bowing, songs of worship, and at times, make animal or human sacrifices on behalf of their belief in what the idol would desire.

Though idolatry is manifested by the building of a physical statue assigned for worship, idolatry can be

**THE WORLD NEEDS THE GIFT THAT ONLY YOU HAS!**

any lustful reverence, or even a fearful reverence of something. For example, when the ants were in the midst of the fire, they fled, but they could have stood in awe at the fire, and its possible danger to them, and remitted their future. When you spend time attaching thoughts of physical perception, it takes time away from the execution of your destiny.

In the transition, you need to take your thoughts captive by remitting negative ideologies and idolatry. Apostle Paul wrote in Romans:

"The one who loves us gives us an overwhelming victory in all these difficulties. I am convinced that nothing can ever separate us from God's love which Christ Jesus our Lord shows us. We can't be separated by death or life, by angels or rulers, by anything in the present or anything in the future, by forces or powers in the world above or in the world below, or by anything else in creation."

3. Formulate a Plan That Protects Your Future

Have you found yourself saying, "I have to stay here because I have a contract, and....", I have to do this because....", and other phrases like that? Let me repeat this again, "Control your thoughts

**REACH YOUR HIGHEST POTENTIAL!**

and ground them in knowledge!". Knowledge has no confines to patterns! Instead of rationalizing your current circumstance, and attempting at silencing your discontentment, you should be coming up with faith based solutions!

You should be saying things like, "I know I have this contract, but this feeling of discontentment is my warning sign that something is out of place, so I am going to ask God for a miracle." God can break any pattern!

I can remember the turmoil that I submitted myself to when I allowed my military obligation to control me. I had surrendered my will on many occasions to the idea that, "I have bills to pay", or, "My son needs…", so I had sacrificed my happiness for commodities. The sacrifice was very disheartening, but when I started to look within at the beauty of how God made me. I started to formulate plans for how I could manifest my dreams. My thoughts went from restraint to a world where I became a partner with God as the author of my future, and my face became brighter. I became overwhelmed with joy in the instant that I chose to have faith in the idea that my dreams can come true.

Would God really pour dreams into you as a tease?

### THE WORLD NEEDS THE GIFT THAT ONLY YOU HAS!

Even if everyone before you had to fulfill their contract or had to accomplish what you feel committed to, God can still re-arrange things so that you can fulfill your purpose for your life.

The longer that you toil in discontentment, the more your imagination is tainted and separated from faith. When you are saying, "I believe in God manifesting this in my life", but you are not connecting your faith to the openness of His timing, it is really an oxymoron, and acting in doubt. You cannot believe that He can, and believe in the sovereignty of your present circumstance at the same time. Do as the ants: acknowledge the circumstance, take your thoughts captive, formulate a plan that protects your future, and EXECUTE!

5. Practice positive self-talk and affirmations that "you can do it!"

As said in The Little Engine That Could, start with, "I think I can", repeat it persistently, and then you will gain the faith to say, "I know I can". Once you know you can, your willpower gains an unforgiving fervor to manifest.

In communication, you can uplift or tear down;

**REACH YOUR HIGHEST POTENTIAL!**

you can encourage or discourage. Communication is a tool that you have that was intended by God as a tool of creation. You have to be careful though because you can create things that appease the ego or the Spirit, and both cannot be satisfied simultaneously.

In The Seven Spiritual Laws Of Success: A Practical Guide to the Fulfillment of Your Dreams, Deepak Chopra says:

"The Ego, however, is not who you really are. The ego is your self-image; it is your social mask; it is the role you are playing. Your social mask thrives on approval. It wants control, and it is sustained by power, because it lives in fear."

If one is ego controlled, his communication is bound to be spiritually poisonous to others; resulting in the creation of thoughts that oppose the Spirit of God. However, if one is as the ant, even in the face of disaster, he will use communication as a way of liberating others.

In the fire, the transmitter ants began laying trails of communication without much time being lost. The chaotic movement of the ant colony began to subside as they had discovered the trail of communication to follow to their next destination, and the colony survived.

In the midst of the fire, rather than surrender, or run off on their own, the ants exercised the power of communication. Communication, whether by body language or by vibrational sound, is a way to disseminate spiritual commerce. Communication is the medium in which we can correct perception and receive knowledge. The Course in Miracles says that knowledge is unchanging, whereas perception is always changing. The ants immediately began communicating about their future. The National Geographic website tells us that ants communicate using chemical trails. They maintain order by having "transmitter ants" assigned to laying communication trails for others to follow. It is unknown if the ant has the ability to communicate perception thoughts such as feelings, emotions, threats, vengeance, and so on. Scientists do know that the ant trail tells the remainder of their colony the route to their future, their nutrients, their purpose, and their safety.

6. Don't try to understand "how"

Your responsibility is not to understand, "how", but to believe. The "how" is the part that you listen for.

## REACH YOUR HIGHEST POTENTIAL!

Be still and meditate. Allow God to tell you the deeds that He requires of you.

I always wanted to be married. As a child, I would play with Barbie dolls; all of which were married. I played house, I had babies, and I watched mothers in awe of the impact that they make on the world.

Due to hardships in relationships, I re-formulated my idea of marriage, and fell prey to the illusion that marriages are not happy. Shortly after, I had reasoned with the philosophy of unhappy marriage, I deployed to Iraq. There, I fell in love with my husband; the man of my dreams. I would have never guessed "how" I would have met him, but neither was that for me to know or understand. Meeting him restored my idea of love and redeemed my philosophy of happy marriage.

As a child, I never wore military garments. I never forecasted a love story where I would be going to war, and meet the man of my dreams, but God had orchestrated the "how". The design of my story meant that I would have the desire of my heart, a husband, but He would design "how".

Your communication should be equally as constructive as that of the ant. It should empower

**THE WORLD NEEDS THE GIFT THAT ONLY YOU HAS!**

and encourage your purpose, and the purpose of those surrounding you.

7. Execute the Plan-DO IT! DO IT! DO IT!

A painful phenomenon occurs in the midst of execution. Your will is tested. You find the physical truth of the spiritual access. In the Spirit or imagination, there is no mass, no pain, no time, no deadlines, and no budget. When you pull the spiritual things into the physical realm, you re-experience the separation that Adam and Eve opened us to in the fall.

Prior to the fall, God walked amongst them, and abundance was of no question. Joy, love, peace, patience, gentleness, and self-control were beyond measure. When Adam and Eve disobeyed God, toil, thorns and thistles became the plot of man for as long until he connects unapologetically and un-relentlessly with the Spirit of God.

Many times the desires that you have created in your imaginations are an appeal to your flesh; they are not required for the subsistence of Spirit. When you are pulling things from the spiritual realm for the edification of our flesh, a painful discipline takes place as you are trying to maintain these commodities. Budgets, time, relational disruption, deadlines, and all these things begin to manifest that feel as if you are facing an uphill climb; the fiercest of discipline. Once you connect the Spirit to the physical manifestation, as Jesus said, "thy Kingdom come on Earth as it is heaven", then the opposition faced as a result of the fall can be overcome. However, this connection with the Spirit is a discipline.

Discipline and commitment are the keys to execution even in terms of connection to the Spirit. Jim Rohn said, "Discipline is the bridge between goals and accomplishment". Most perceive discipline with the ideology of pain and struggle, but discipline is merely consistency in building towards a goal. The discipline required for connection with the Spirit is consistency in prayer, meditation, and stillness. The discipline required for other manifestation adjoined with joy, peace, patience, gentleness, kindness, and self-control in the midst of the execution is consistent progression alongside fragments of inner stillness, and thoughts of possibility (re-affirming ones' potential).

Consistent progression is the most difficult practice for most people to master, but it is pertinent to execution. Consistency means that regardless

**THE WORLD NEEDS THE GIFT THAT ONLY YOU HAS!**

of circumstance, you will execute a task on a recurring basis. Darren Hardy said," "Since your outcomes are all a result of your moment-to-moment choices, you have incredible power to change your life by changing those choices. Step by step, day by day, your choices will shape your actions until they become habits, where practice makes them permanent." On another occasion in his book The Compound Effect he said, " "Small, Smart Choices + Consistency + Time = RADICAL DIFFERENCE".

**REACH YOUR HIGHEST POTENTIAL!**

## PERCEPTION EXERCISE

Write down present areas of discontentment in your life:

|   |
|---|
|   |
|   |
|   |
|   |
|   |
|   |
|   |

Write down thoughts that come to mind when you experience discontentment:

|   |
|---|
|   |
|   |
|   |
|   |
|   |
|   |
|   |

Maintaining positive self-talk will be vital to your success in any area of your life. For this exercise,

**THE WORLD NEEDS THE GIFT THAT ONLY YOU HAS!**

you need to write twelve positive affirmations. We want you to replace attack, vulnerability, and discontentment. Example: I am beautiful. I am fully equipped for my purpose.

# CHAPTER THREE: THE POWER OF LOVE

What we think is good, bad, biblical, non-biblical, right, wrong, tastes good or not is entirely based upon our perception. Meaningless means not worth clenching or holding onto. Meaningless is alleviated from expectation. Meaningless is dissolved from universal perception and value. Meaningless means entirely defined by ones' perception. Everything has its meaning because of our own defining process, but you cannot be defined by man because your value and definition has already been set in place by God.

The Bible says that you are made in the image of God. And in a different passage it says that, "God is love". When combined, you can summarize that you are made in the image of love, and therefore should be reflecting it without limitations. God created us to need connection to create new human form. Unlimited, unhindered, unconditional love is called, agape. Agape love is beyond our flesh, our desires, and covers over wrong. Love can be felt without words. In the midst of many languages; love can transcend the language barriers. Love is the medium whereby all atoms are formulated into objects,

## THE WORLD NEEDS THE GIFT THAT ONLY YOU HAS!

and it is the only explanation for creation and life. Without love, the universe has no purpose; the sun has no reason to shine, the trees have no reason to bear fruit, nor does the water have any reason to replenish. Love can be felt as the strongest vibration; superior to the vibrations of sound, superior to the physical vibrations that manifest in a storm. Love is universal and can be felt simultaneously across the Earth.

Your purpose on this Earth is beyond yourself and self-esteem and inner exaltation is unnecessary when you understand that you are the image of God. You need to have the fervor and the strong focus on your own highest potential in life. Your purpose is not replaceable, that is why you are here. If someone else could accomplish your role, you would not be created. God created you to His satisfaction; which is perfection in every rite.

The Bible tells us to go to the ant to find wisdom, something worth far greater than gold or silver. God is even mindful of a being as small as the ant; providing them abundance in everything that they could possibly need. How much more do you think God desires to do this for you?

You were made with a value that man cannot

**REACH YOUR HIGHEST POTENTIAL!**

equate with currency. God assigned you a greater value than the Earth and everything that we see, which is why He chose to spare man even in instances like the flood where He cleared the Earth of every living thing (animals, plants, and people included). He still saw fit to spare Noah and thru him came you.

Some may deny the presence of love, but when they are absent of their blindness just by simply inquiring of God, one can find that their purpose is love; not for themselves, but the love and impact of others as Jesus emulated and pointed out 2000+ years ago. Jesus is the physical symbol of the phenomenon that had spiritually been known and felt as love.

When I have felt at my loneliest, when I was child-rearing my young baby. I used to be overwhelmed by thoughts of possible inadequacy and thoughts that I would not be able to recuperate my sleep, and on and on. I never had a baby in my care before. I was learning how to address each cry, but it was new, and sometimes heart-wrenching. My closest family member was 30+ hours driving distance. His father never seemed to have many pleasant things to say to me. I was new to the Air Force, and resistant at sharing my concerns because

## THE WORLD NEEDS THE GIFT THAT ONLY YOU HAS!

I didn't want to be perceived as "dramatic".

I remember several instances where I had nowhere to turn. I needed love. In these instances, I would sit, close my eyes, allow my mind to wonder into complete solitude, and repeat the name "Jesus".

In the article, The Mysticism of Sound, it talks about the power of repetition. By repeating a phrase, we can affect the vibrations around us that create our environments. With certain tested and tried words, we can create different environments.

Jesus lived his life to love and to serve. He died to love and to serve, and He conquered death thru love. The Father did not allow Him to die an eternal death, but instead restored Him to the fullness of the Spirit of God which surrounds each of us. The same spirit infiltrates your lungs as you breath in and out. The same Spirit quenches your thirst as you drink. Just thru closing my eyes and allowing the vibrational intensity of my mouth repeat the name of Jesus, allowing the visualization of his love to the world infiltrate my mind, would alleviate my loneliness.

I would realize that I am still purposed to be here. He would not provide for me if I were not sup-

## REACH YOUR HIGHEST POTENTIAL!

posed to be here. His Spirit keeps the vibrational intensity within my body; my heart beat, my eyes blinking, my blood pacing thru my veins. I am embraced by the Spirit of God in every way.

Thru his actions of encouraging, generosity, healing, deliverance, giving life, and expanding our imaginations to understand our potential, Jesus has had more of an impact than every being that has ever walked the face of the Earth. Jesus sent of the greatest vibrations of love; penetrating the souls of those who had created barriers of hate. The vibrations of love that Jesus sent off are unending, they projected and returned to their source to continue to recycle their trail for times unending. Because of his immense unparalleled love, He is the display and the bridge for all to emulate the necessary love that it requires to connect with God. Without the love that was shown by His presence and impact in the world, our imaginations could not contain the possibility of being so effective as to reach 100% of humanity with the aspiration of selflessness. Our imaginations were not capable to fathom the ideology that we could influence people in such a way as to create an aspiration of such volume and intimacy. For this reason, Jesus is the only way and the savior. He is the ONE that has exemplified a legacy of 2000+ years of followers who aspire to

## THE WORLD NEEDS THE GIFT THAT ONLY YOU HAS!

love others to a precedent that has never before or since been seen. His reflection of God (Love) that no one has yet to supersede, but that is required to achieve holiness and achieve eternity is the reason that Jesus is the savior and the greatest mentor of all time.

The strength of the vibrations of love that you show can reverse the patterns of time, can heal, and can save someone from death. Jesus demonstrated power over time, space, natural laws, and death in His life as he performed miracles that exemplified how love cannot be contained. If you extend the greatest empathy and faith, you can conquer all things. For this reason the Bible says, "I can do all things thru Christ who gives me strength". Absent from your ego, you should be able to understand the unity and connection of the universe. The trees release oxygen, living beings inhale oxygen, and though it does not have a physical mass, you must understand the connection of the universe to you. Thru this spiritual and physical connection, you are connected thru everything that you take in and release. Everything that you take into your body, releases in a different form that increases the quality for the next being. The "ecosystem phenomenon" is designed in love; connecting all beings to each other and to their Source.

**REACH YOUR HIGHEST POTENTIAL!**

The beginning of truly having power in love is to understand your tools to display it. God demonstrated to us how we are supposed to show love with the things He has given us.

**THE WORLD NEEDS THE GIFT THAT ONLY YOU HAS!**

## PERCEPTION EXERCISE

Do you get upset when someone eats your food, calls you names, or what is it that "pushes your button"? With this exercise, we want to remove conditions to our love, and step closer to Agape. Write down 10 ways that you can remove conditions from your love towards others.

**REACH YOUR HIGHEST POTENTIAL!**

# CHAPTER FOUR: THE POWER OF YOUR STORY

Beyond our collective purpose to encourage and exhort, we have personal responsibilities to make transformation in the Earth before the Kingdom comes on Earth. Know, your purpose must be fulfilled. The reason you are on this Earth was to fulfill a duty.

Your purpose can be manifested in many ways, but all of these ways are attached to your unique abilities, areas of mastery, and you story. You are valuable to everyone on the Earth.

The story is a recollection of your successes and failures. It is the route to arrive to where you are.

The ants remember their route. They ensure that they don't loose their route by placing chemical trails on the ground. When they are ready to return or to lead others to the newfound destination for food or whatever it is they have found, they lead them along the trails that they have laid.

Your trail is your story. It leads others to where

## THE WORLD NEEDS THE GIFT THAT ONLY YOU HAS!

you are. It teaches others of traps to avoid, and empowers them because you are still here.

In my childhood, I was able to witness other children in abusive situations at school. I was a child from a fairly painless childhood. My parents have been happily married all of my life, which gave my siblings and I much accountability and stability. They dually parented us; if one parent assigned us to do a task, the other would assist in ensuring that we had accomplished the task. Additionally, they supported the spiritual growth and development of one another, which constantly provided the support that they both needed to be financially privileged as well. My siblings and I genuinely loved one another. We had our moments, but the prevailing summary that everyone could gain is that we loved one another. Our family predominantly wore smiles, we vacationed together, we celebrated holidays and birthdays together, we always knew that our important events would not be spent alone because we always have been a family full of love.

Seeing others around me that did not have such a joyous way to tell their childhood story made me question the value in mine. I would hear rape and molestation stories, child trauma, adultery and affair stories, and because I was not a participant,

## REACH YOUR HIGHEST POTENTIAL!

firsthand witness, or victim of such an event, I thought that my story held less value. When we would do testimonies at church, I remember being shy to share my blissful stories because I felt that I needed to have a story that began with trauma, something that I had done incredibly wrong, or a near death situation where God had saved me. I had lessened the value of my story by escalating the value in the stories of others.

Later, I learned that the story tells another person a possibility. Your story has the power to increase another's' imagination and faith, so much that it becomes a possibility in their mind. When I heard the stories of rape and molestation, my story could have been enlightening to the possibility that others may not experience that. Simultaneously, the same stories were an eye-opener to me because even now, I have not witnessed or experienced some of the activities in the stories that I'd heard.

Scientists have done lab testing to confirm the power of storytelling. When two people are brought together, they use different parts of their brains to interpret the present circumstance. Lab testing shows that if one person begins telling a story that both brains become in sync, and they begin both using the same portions of the brain to

## THE WORLD NEEDS THE GIFT THAT ONLY YOU HAS!

share the story and to receive the story. Storytelling literally syncs two minds to one cause.

Additionally, if you have observed people that are able to capture and sustain large audiences, the number one strategy for accomplishing this task is thru storytelling. For example, Dr. Yonggi Cho, pastor of the world's largest congregation of one million+ members leads his weekly services with prayers, but as he is preaching, he tells stories. His stories are so compelling as to engage a continual audience of one million + members, while also sustaining millions of nonmembers internationally thru Livestream. The same tactics are used for America's largest gatherings of viewers: the TED talks, the Oprah Winfrey Show, Joel Osteen's church, Liberty University, and others. Storytelling is a medium of tuning two minds to one note. Storytelling makes harmony amongst strangers and familiar people alike.

The hidden benefit that you have is that your story is unique. Even if you have a very close family, there are differences in your story than everyone else. Your unique story is valuable and should be shared to liberate others! You are the message of liberation to others!

**REACH YOUR HIGHEST POTENTIAL!**

A vital part of the liberation process is vulnerability, and the most vulnerable form is nakedness. Spiritually, your story, your talents, and your unique identifiers strengthen your stature. When you are spiritually unsheathed, you have the most opportunity to liberate others.

Spiritual openness means that you release yourself from the ideas of shame connected with certain passages in your life story and replace the designation with triumph. However, you must share the experience before the triumph with discretion and guide listeners to the outcome.

The ability to openly share your talents and your story is the beginning to your success. The next part to your success, is releasing your talents and your story to be shared with as many others as can possibly receive it.

For most, visibility is attached to fear or some selfish negative "don't want" perspective. "I don't want to be in front of a lot of people", "I don't want to pay money to record myself", "I don't want people to try to get over on me", "I don't have enough time", and more excuses roll on. Instead, you should be focused on the outcome to the majority, which in essence is the core of your purpose: to

**THE WORLD NEEDS THE GIFT THAT ONLY YOU HAS!**

uplift others.

You must surrender yourself wholly to God, and the ways that He desires you to be used for the sake of others. He has temporarily given you value by way of your life story and talents, so that He can see how well you make use of them. Will you multiply them? Will you exhort others and encourage them to reach their highest potential? If your answer is "yes", you can assuredly know that you will pass the test.

**REACH YOUR HIGHEST POTENTIAL!**

## PERCEPTION EXERCISE

1. What is your unique story?

2. Are you grateful for your story? Do you use it to benefit and uplift others?

3. What do you do to make money?

4. What are your talents or areas of mastery?

5. What limitations does the Bible say that you have?

6. What limitations do you believe that you have?

7. Do you start this pursuit to make money because you believe that it is your life's purpose or because you feel obligated?

8. Your legacy is what houses your Spirit after you have left the Earth. What do you actively pursue to increase your legacy?

9. Have you participated in impulsive things to appease your emotions or your ego?

**THE WORLD NEEDS THE GIFT THAT ONLY YOU HAS!**

11. Where do you gain direction? Do you find yourself saying, "My mom told me to…..", "My friend told me to", "My dad told me to", or other similar statements?

12. What would be your one word definition of money?
Tip: Your description of money tells us whether you believe that value is a renewable or easily accessed resource or not. Security, Stability, tell us that you need to focus on building spiritually in wisdom. Money is not a spiritual resource, but it is the physical sign of wisdom. If you lack money, in the Spirit, you must ask for Wisdom.

13. Describe your perception influences:

14. Describe common perception influences around you:

15. Describe wisdom sources:

16. Provide an action plan to increase your wisdom intake:

## REACH YOUR HIGHEST POTENTIAL!

11. Where do you gain direction? Do you find yourself saying, "My mom told me to…..", "My friend told me to", "My dad told me to", or other similar statements?

12. What would be your one word definition of money?
Tip: Your description of money tells us whether you believe that value is a renewable or easily accessed resource or not. Security, Stability, tell us that you need to focus on building spiritually in wisdom. Money is not a spiritual resource, but it is the physical sign of wisdom. If you lack money, in the Spirit, you must ask for Wisdom.

13. Describe your perception influences:

14. Describe common perception influences around you:

15. Describe wisdom sources:

16. Provide an action plan to increase your wisdom intake:

## AFFIRMATIONS

## THE WORLD NEEDS THE GIFT THAT ONLY YOU HAS!

I am grateful for my access.
I am grateful for what I have
Abundance is all around me
I will use everything that I have to advance my purpose.
I am valuable to everyone.
A good idea is currency from Heaven
Satan desires to steal, kill, and destroy my potential

**REACH YOUR HIGHEST POTENTIAL!**

# CHAPTER FIVE: THE BODY, YOUR TEMPORAL RESIDENCE

Our bodies were designed to be creative. We create goodness and things that can stimulate further inspiration and closeness to God.

We were designed to hug, to kiss, to have sex, to hold hands, and all these things are initiated by good ideas. Alternatively, the Kingdom of Darkness uses the same good things to inspire bad things. God orchestrated a context for each of these uses of the body, but sometimes, we allow our perception of what He said to rule. We say things like, "He said that in the Old Testament", or, "That is not today's culture", when rather, God is the Beginning and the End; creation until the Earth passes away. Therefore, modern perceptions and thoughts cannot be permitted to outweigh the King. In an Earthly Kingdom, trends cannot outweigh laws, why do we permit this with the most longstanding Kingdom known to man?

The ant was created with their skeleton on the outside called, an exoskeleton. Their structure protects them from the outside in rather than the human

**THE WORLD NEEDS THE GIFT THAT ONLY YOU HAS!**

structure where our bones are internal.

God has given us the responsibility and choice to protect our bodies from the outside in. Our diets, our dress, our relationships, our media intake, etc., all must be guarded from the outside in.

> **"Honor your spiritual body and treat it with discretion, love, and virtue."**

The physical body is a symbol. It symbolizes your spiritual body (which is sizable beyond measure); it is the structure that we are supposed to be in relationships. Each limb, organ, and part is connected, and required for maximum health. Parts of the body are used to gather nutrients, to communicate, to travel, and so on. For this reason Apostle Paul said:

For just as the body is a unity and yet has many parts, and all the parts, though many, form [only] one body, so it is with Christ (the Messiah, the Anointed One). For by means of the personal agency of] one [Holy] Spirit we were all, whether Jews or Greeks, slaves or free, baptized [and By baptism united together] into one body, and all made to drink of one [Holy] Spirit. For the body does not consist of one limb *or* organ but of many. If the foot should say, Because I am not the hand, I do not belong to the body, would it be therefore not [a part] of the body?

**REACH YOUR HIGHEST POTENTIAL!**

If the ear should say, Because I am not the eye, I do not belong to the body, would it be therefore not [a part] of the body? If the whole body were an eye, where [would be the sense of] hearing? If the whole body were an ear, where [would be the sense of] smell?

But as it is, God has placed *and* arranged the limbs *and* organs in the body, each [particular one] of them, just as He wished *and* saw fit *and* with the best adaptation. But if [the whole] were all a single organ, where would the body be? And now there are [certainly] many limbs *and* organs, but a single body. And the eye is not able to say to the hand, I have no need of you, nor again the head to the feet, I have no need of you. But instead, there is [absolute] necessity for the parts of the body that are considered the more weak. And those [parts] of the body which we consider rather ignoble are [the very parts] which we invest with additional honor, and our unseemly parts *and* those unsuitable for exposure are treated with seemliness (modesty and decorum), Which our more presentable parts do not require. But God has so adjusted (mingled, harmonized, and subtly proportioned the parts of) the whole body, giving the greater honor *and* richer endowment to the inferior parts which lack [apparent importance], So that there should be no division *or* discord *or* lack of adaptation [of the parts

**THE WORLD NEEDS THE GIFT THAT ONLY YOU HAS!**

of the body to each other], but the members all alike should have a mutual interest in *and* care for one another. (1 Corinthians 12:12-27 Amplified)

The body functions together, and does not expose the faults or malfunctions of its parts. For example, in a business setting, when someone incidentally passes gas, the person does not usually proclaim, "I passed gas!" amongst the crowd, but instead silently ignores the movement in hopes that no one will notice.

The same is supposed to be true of our relationship to others as the body, and the same is true of the discretion that we should have with our physical bodies.

When we seek the ants for wisdom, we see that the colony is collaboration. Ants are never alone. When they are removed from their colony and displaced, they immediately search to restore their communion with their colony. Their assignment is to one colony. Their target audience is only them.

Your spiritual body is your team; the collaboration of Kingdom citizens across the globe. The unfortunate failure of most people is lacking knowledge. In ignorance, they do not make use of the edifice of the church, but rather project offense onto the

## REACH YOUR HIGHEST POTENTIAL!

church because the place the church in the position of their Provider.

Many people go to church with the thought that this is the disciplined time that I have set aside for God, and expect that they will receive direction from the church. The church is supposed to be the ministry of each person in attendance; not a place where perfection lives, but a place that needs you to stabilize, uplift, and play your God-given role. We (the Church, the Bride of Christ) need you because "honey is coming home soon!"

Many people do not see that they are supposed to be a productive part of the body, and instead of looking for fault, they should be concealing it. The church has lost the reputation of sanctity because of the critics within her. In a metaphorical sense, the church passes gas, defecates, sweats, and manifests other things that may not look or smell so inviting, which is why we need you to provide the nutrients to balance her, clean her, and uplift her, so we can be prepared for the return of Jesus. We are a collection of sinners joined to receive redemption from God, and you have a part. You may find a person that steps on your toes, that tells you something wrong, that may e\be adulterous, and so on, but use what you have to make the difference; become the move-

**THE WORLD NEEDS THE GIFT THAT ONLY YOU HAS!**

ment that you want to see.

My friend told me a story of when she went to the hospital. An elderly man collapsed at the front door. Doctors and nurses passed him by concerned about liability and being to work on time, and no one would help. My friend, who has no emergency experience called the emergency line, and waited with the man for an ambulance.

What happened to the collapsed man happens all the time in the church; a tragedy. People see something obviously wrong; a person that they notice is defying God, and without grace or tact, they either pursue the person very judgmentally or leave and criticize the entire body. Be the movement that you want to see! Act as if the person acting badly is you passing gas in public, and treat them with grace. The Bible shows the consequence of the grace that we should show the body when it says:

-Hatred stirs up contentions, but love covers all transgressions. (Proverbs 10:10)

-He who covers *and* forgives an offense seeks love, but he who repeats *or* harps on a matter separates even close friends. (Proverbs 17:9)

# REACH YOUR HIGHEST POTENTIAL!

-Above all things have intense *and* unfailing love for one another, for love covers a multitude of sins [forgives and disregards the offenses of others]. (1 Peter 4:8)

**"Treat your physical body with modesty and diligence."**

Lacking discretion with your body ruins your reputation. For this reason, Jesus said:

"Do not give that which is holy (the sacred thing) to the dogs, and do not throw your pearls before hogs, lest they trample upon them with their feet and turn *and* tear you in pieces."

Your body is the physical encasement of your spirit, and it changes. You evolve from a baby's corpse to whatever corpse is fitting for the age that you depart the Earth. Your physical body is given to you with purpose.

Gender Identity has become a huge topic of dispute. People say that they were born feeling like the opposite gender of that which they were born physically. The reason for this is that the Spirit within a person has no gender. We are participants in the creation process here on Earth, but God is the ultimate decision maker regarding the gender

**THE WORLD NEEDS THE GIFT THAT ONLY YOU HAS!**

that we come. It is easy for physical beings to desire to manifest traits other than their own, however, your physical gender identity is a part of your purpose.

I have been given the body of a woman. Sometimes, I exercise male personality traits. I admire beauty regardless of gender. I have shown strength when performing tasks that are typical of men, but none of my masculine qualities gives me the authority to transform my body, or use my body apart from the directions that the Manufacturer has set.

Dishes that are dishwasher safe should not be put in the dishwasher whether they can fit or not. They should not go in the dishwasher even if it appears to be good for them or not damaging them because the Manufacturer knows the detriment to the dishes far ahead in the future than we do.

The size and shape of your features is a part of your purpose. God has enabled you to reach the people necessary to your purpose by assigning you the body that you have. You may be small, big, purple, green, you may consider that you have ailments or disabilities, but they are not seen that way in God's eyes; they are a part of your assignment. Your assignment does not entitle you to transform what

## REACH YOUR HIGHEST POTENTIAL!

is not yours. Your body is not yours; it is a temple made by God for God. It is not you. It is a tool for you to manifest detriment to the world. Wayne Dyer said, "You cannot always control what goes on outside. However you can always control what goes on inside." Your dominion is to control your thoughts towards the body.

I listened to a mother tell me the story of her baby being born with no gallbladder, and pooping white stools. She thought, "Why would God give me a dysfunctional baby? Why wouldn't He give me a baby that operated normally?"

We are all guilty of thinking like this mother had. The norms are our expectations. We do not expect the groundbreaking liberation that can come to others when life is outside the norm.

She prayed for her baby, got the best healthcare that she could find, and when the doctors declared that the baby would die, she prayed with the utmost passion. Her heart cry was heard by God, her baby began pooping brown stools. His liver was restored to full function. X-rays had been performed at many of America's top hospitals, and when the doctors were searching for the scientific cause of her baby's liver going from inoperable to completely restored, they found a healthy liver, and

**THE WORLD NEEDS THE GIFT THAT ONLY YOU HAS!**

a healthy gallbladder. God had birthed two miracles in this child: restoration of the liver, and the miraculous placement of a gallbladder that was not there before.

As a result of the miracle with the baby, the mother said that her faith was increased, her husband began to recognize that God exits, her children have unshakeable faith, and the doctors (void of an explanation) were embedded with a seed of curiosity. He used this baby to show that God is not contained in patterns, and what you think is a dysfunction can be a tool for the liberation of many.

Your body was created "good" just the way that you got it, and when it operates outside of the manufacturers details (The Bible), and you are submitted to the Kingdom laws, you petition the Kingdom of Heaven to manifest your Kingdom rights, and God will do just as He said He would. Jesus told us of our power to manifest the things of Heaven when He said:

I will give you the keys of the kingdom of heaven; and whatever you bind (declare to be improper and unlawful) on earth must be what is already bound in heaven; and whatever you loose (declare lawful) on earth must be what is already loosed in heaven.

We know the Kingdom does not have sickness, nor conflict, nor lack, or discomfort, but instead it is the storehouse of abundance and perfection. Therefore, when you are manifesting something that is inconsistent with the attributes of the Kingdom, and you have submitted yourselves to Kingdom laws, you can petition the Kingdom. Jesus told us to pray that the Kingdom would come, and He would not say so of it were not possible. The Kingdom can be manifested in your body thru restored health, the Kingdom can be manifested in your home thru protection, peace, and abundance. As Jesus said, "The Kingdom is at hand!" The Kingdom is among us, and can be manifested whenever we petition the Manufacturer of our lives.

Dr. Myles Munroe described that God operates as manufacturers do. They always send their merchandise with directions and warranties. When the product malfunctions within the confines of the warranty, you can tell the manufacturer, and they will coordinate a suitable agreement for the sake of their name.

The same is true of God. Our bodies are

**THE WORLD NEEDS THE GIFT THAT ONLY YOU HAS!**

supposed to operate as defined in the Bible. When they do not, you can report the concern to Him. You say, "Your Word says that my body is supposed to _____, and right now it is _____. I am bringing this concern before you, the manufacturer of my body and my life, and giving you access. I am assured that I have access to health because your word says of the Kingdom that God would wipe away every tear from our eyes; and death shall be no more, neither shall there be anguish (sorrow and mourning) nor grief nor pain any more, for the old conditions *and* the former order of things have passed away. I ask that your Kingdom would come, and make my body operate according to my Kingdom rights in Jesus name. Amen.

The illusion that our body requires chemical alterations for beauty is not true. Not only has God given us the bodies that He desired for us to have, but He also yields us the direction of how to use our plant resources and wisdom of others to heal our bodies if you just ask.

In Someone Covets You, Sin said, "I tell Woman, You are ugly! You have to cover your outrageous skin outbreaks!" Instead of running away from me, she runs towards me, and requests my help. Then, I use magic to transform her face. If honesty is what you desire, I will give you a dose....

**REACH YOUR HIGHEST POTENTIAL!**

I HATE YOU AND I HATE MANKIND. I tell my daughter to make man and woman look like I beat them, like they are dying, burning, or simply suffering. She puts black, purple, orange, and all other colors on her face to conceal that she looks like the Father.

Why should they be beautiful? I should be the only beauty. I have recalibrated their minds to desire the things that avail to me. Think about it, why else would Man and Woman like markings of bones, red lipstick, and black eye shadow? I want them to look as if they were beat and lifeless. As with all other tasks, I have directed the sheep into the belief of an ulterior view of physical beauty.

The Father wanted Man to see beauty in virtuous characteristics and to befriend Wisdom beyond all others. He portrayed beauty as love, joy, peace, patience, kindness, gentleness, and self-control. He wanted man to be attuned to the sight of virtuous character thru modesty, humility, diligence, confidence, productivity, dignity, use of discretion in decision-making, generosity, preparation, attentive listening, receptiveness to instruction, and other attributes that the eye can perceive.

Can't you tell a confident person in their stride, or in their tactful dress? Can't you tell a dil-

**THE WORLD NEEDS THE GIFT THAT ONLY YOU HAS!**

igent person in the cleanliness of their bodies, and in how well they groom themselves? The Father wanted Man to ally with people of noble character, but on the contrary, he preferred me. Regardless of the plans of the Father, humanity has not preserved their minds, but rather has left the minds as instruments for me to play the melodies that I desire to hear."

Be grateful for the purpose that you have been assigned thru your body. Your pain is temporary, your thoughts towards it are under your dominion, and satisfaction with your body is your choice.

Your senses and your feelings should not be in control of your body, but rather your body should be submitted to the purpose of your assignment. If you know that you have been assigned to do something, you must know that Satan may send the kingdom of darkness to oppose your assignment. For this reason, Paul said:

For we are not wrestling with flesh and blood [contending only with physical opponents], but against the despotisms, against the powers, against [the master spirits who are] the world rulers of this present darkness, against the spirit forces of wickedness in the heavenly (supernatural) sphere. (Ephesians 6:12)

Your body works at your command, and when you feel that you need additional support, you petition Heaven. The King can relinquish miracles in your life or send the angels to ally with you. Just ask!

**THE WORLD NEEDS THE GIFT THAT ONLY YOU HAS!**

## PERCEPTION EXERCISE

Write down 10 positive uses of your body just the way that it is:

1. My body is good at/for_____

2. My body is good at/for_____

3. My body is good at/for_____

4. My body is good at/for_____

5. My body is good at/for_____

6. My body is good at/for_____

7. My body is good at/for_____

8. My body is good at/for_____

9. My body is good at/for_____

10. My body is good at/for_____

Write down 5 ways that the Kingdom Ambassadors (your spiritual body) are positively used around you:

## REACH YOUR HIGHEST POTENTIAL!

Write down 5 ways that you can use your talents to add to the positive things that are happening amongst your Royal Lineage (Kingdom brothers and sisters).

**THE WORLD NEEDS THE GIFT THAT ONLY YOU HAS!**

# CHAPTER SIX:
# THE POWER OF IDEAS

Ideas are spiritual currency. Until you understand that ideas are the resource that supplies your needs and wants, you will be undervaluing them. King Solomon said, "How much better it is to get skillful *and* godly Wisdom than gold! And to get understanding is to be chosen rather than silver."

Wisdom is worth more than money! Sound ideas come from God. Pastor Benny Hinn asked Dr. Myles Munroe in an interview, "How do you know when visions come from God?" He responded, "Visions from God are not for you alone." To take it a step further, ideas from God are not for you alone. God inspires ideas that benefit many.

As a recipient of ideas, it is your responsibility to: (1) Manifest the idea, and, (2) Place the manifestation before the people that need it. Both byproducts of an idea; manifestation and marketing require submission from the recipient, but obedience yields great fruit!

Some will manifest the idea and offer the byproduct at billions of dollars, while others with self-limiting beliefs will offer the manifestation for little or no charge. It is the choice of the recipient; a grace granted by God. The seriousness that you take ideas directly correlates to the comforts that you have, how you live, and the generosity that you can display.

When an idea is taken with high esteem, the recipient will do their best to ensure that it reaches the maximum amount of people in his or her power. Jesus spoke of the process of fishing for men. The responsibility to fish was assigned to all of his followers. As fishermen, we should be attempting to catch many fish, which means that we will need a large net. The larger the net and the more receptive to the Father, the more success in catching fish, and the more value to the manifestation.

After Jesus died, he appeared on several occasions to his disciples and others in Israel. When he first resurrected, he brought many from the grave with him. On one occasion, his disciples, Peter, Thomas, and Nathaniel were fishing. Peter was a professional fisherman before walking with Jesus. The Bible does not say, but it is possible that since Jesus had not yet relinquished His Spirit amongst them that their ministry was a discouragement without him. Whatever the case, the disciples decided to pursue something that they thought that they could do in their own strength. They fished all night with-

## THE WORLD NEEDS THE GIFT THAT ONLY YOU HAS!

out catching fish, and when Jesus appeared, it was morning.

"So Jesus said to them, Boys (children), you do not have any meat (fish), do you? [Have you caught anything to eat along with your bread?] They answered Him, No! And He said to them, Cast the net on the right side of the boat and you will find [some]. So they cast the net, and now they were not able to haul it in for such a big catch (mass, quantity) of fish [was in it]. Then the disciple whom Jesus loved said to Peter, It is the Lord! Simon Peter, hearing him say that it was the Lord, put (girded) on his upper garment (his fisherman's coat, his outer tunic)—for he was stripped [for work]—and sprang into the sea. And the other disciples came in the small boat, for they were not far from shore, only some hundred yards away, dragging the net full of fish. When they got out on land (the beach), they saw a fire of coals there and fish lying on it [cooking], and bread. Jesus said to them, Bring some of the fish which you have just caught. So Simon Peter went aboard and hauled the net to land, full of large fish, 153 of them; and [though] there were so many of them, the net was not torn."

When we are receptive to the ideas of God, He can plant ideas that supply us what we need. He can expedite whatever we are trying to receive. He will teach us how to fish, so that we can meet the people

**REACH YOUR HIGHEST POTENTIAL!**

of whom we are assigned, and bless the giver and the receiver for being obedient in the transaction.

Everything manifested on Earth began with an idea. Nothing begins on Earth. King Solomon said, "There is nothing new under the sun". The inspiration is planted in the mind from the spiritual realm. Currency is placed in the account (mind), and withdrawn by the persistent action of the body in submission to God. For example, when the disciples were fishing. The currency (idea) to fish had been planted in their minds, and their submission to the direction of Jesus gained them their withdraw or (results).

Ideas are abundant, but time on Earth is not. Therefore, each idea should be entitled to swift responsiveness. If an idea was assigned to you and you chose not to manifest it, or disseminate it to those who needed it, it leaves the Earth without the benefit that it was entitled.

When disaster hits the Earth, it is because we are CO-creators submitting to our flesh and the Kingdom of Darkness. When lack hits the Earth, it is because we are CO-creators. When we choose not to deposit the currency of the Spirit to those who were assigned to receive it, it leaves others abandoned of the prosperity that God assigned to them.

**THE WORLD NEEDS THE GIFT THAT ONLY YOU HAS!**

"People generally fall into one of three groups: the few who make things happen, the many who watch things happen, and the overwhelming majority who have no notion of what happens. Every person is either a creator of fact or a creature of circumstance. He either puts color into his environment, or, like a chameleon, takes color from his environment... You must decide if you are going to rob the world or bless it with the rich, valuable, potent, untapped resources locked away within you." (Munroe 1991)

**"Do not let the grave get wealthier with your untapped ideas!"**

Similar to how sound ideas can increase you, submission to a poor source of insight can also cause your demise. It is VITAL to your life potential that you be in the constant surveillance. Your future is encapsulated in three things: your legacy, your creation (writing, painting, entertaining, singing, etc.), and most importantly, your imagination. You protect your future by being watchful of the people that you keep around you and the things that you allow to affect your senses.

Although the ants are surrounded with plenty, they are mindful of what they bring into their colony. Grass-eating ants do not go out of their colonies and select the first blade of grass. Instead, they travel to find the best blade for their colony.

**REACH YOUR HIGHEST POTENTIAL!**

The same concept is true with sifting between good and bad ideas. We have to discern the origin of the idea. When an idea comes, you must ask yourself, "Who is the author of this idea? Is it God, my flesh, or Satan? Will this benefit my purpose and others or not?"

**"Bad ideas can cause you to wander from purpose."**

At eighteen, I had succumbed to the cultural norm of being "grown" because of my age. I demanded independence. My parents were still desiring to participate in raising me; telling me that they would pay for me to go to college full-time as long as I did not work. Their ultimatum overwhelmed me because I could not fathom the idea of wanting something, and having to ask permission for it. I was grown. I still wanted to go to school, and I still wanted amenities, so I searched for jobs that would allow me to balance my desires with my paycheck.

I am an artist, so I thought working at a nail shop might work, and I went to cosmetology school. After I completed my schooling, I interned at a Vietnamese nail shop where I learned the tricks of the trade. I could apply acrylic and gel nails

**THE WORLD NEEDS THE GIFT THAT ONLY YOU HAS!**

with mastery, painting designs seemed to flow naturally, the nail shop had its own regular flow of clientele that I would service, and customer service was a joy. Despite the success I was having, within a short time, I discovered that working at the nail shop would take a great deal of time to meet my goals. It was a time-consuming service, so I decided to get a second job working at McDonald's.

I really enjoyed McDonald's! It was a very social environment. I had the opportunity to cheer people up as I would hand them their meal in the drive thru and say, "Have a great day!". The drive-thru was my favorite; I had the chance to interact with several people consistently.

It had been one semester in school, and working two jobs became exhausting. Paying for my school was very difficult even with all of my time invested in working, so I began to explore more options. I was looking into being a truck driver. I perceived that the benefits would be great. "Medical coverage, dental coverage, and travel?", I said, "I can't beat that!". I started to investigate what I would need to do to be a truck driver.

I began preparing myself for a new experience when one day, I was glancing thru the newspaper. I saw an ad that said, "$40,000.00 sign-on bonus for a cook".

## REACH YOUR HIGHEST POTENTIAL!

I said, "This is it! I can cook and go to school". I called the number, and the respondent requested that I come in for an appointment. Upon my arrival, I noticed that it was an Army recruiter. Until this point, I had never considered the military. I was extremely feminine in my tendencies, so it was difficult for me to visualize how I could fit my personality into the uniform, but I decided to give it a shot.

I listened to the recruiter, and went back to seek advice from my family. My Aunt Joyce is in the Army, and had prior Air Force experience, so we talked about the pros and cons of each. We decided that my desires were more compatible with the Air Force, so I went to the Air Force recruiter, and left for Basic Military Training within ten days.

Within six months of leaving for the Air Force, I became pregnant, and within one year of my departure from home, I was a single mom. Thereafter, I began learning some very adult lessons. It was my journey as a nineteen year old single mom that taught me a WHOLE lot about protecting our futures.

Embedded throughout childhood was a self-limiting belief that going to school and working hard led to success. I had not seen a person who stepped from my modest life, pursued certain disciplines, and therefore succeeded. Somewhere, deeply plant-

**THE WORLD NEEDS THE GIFT THAT ONLY YOU HAS!**

ed within, I had the belief that rich people either "got lucky", "knew the right people", or "Did something wrong".

Bad ideas are those that are stimulated by the fruits of the flesh:
It is obvious what kind of life develops out of trying to get your own way all the time: repetitive, loveless, cheap sex; a stinking accumulation of mental and emotional garbage; frenzied and joyless grabs for happiness; trinket gods; magic-show religion; paranoid loneliness; cutthroat competition; all-consuming-yet-never-satisfied wants; a brutal temper; an impotence to love or be loved; divided homes and divided lives; small-minded and lopsided pursuits; the vicious habit of depersonalizing everyone into a rival; uncontrolled and uncontrollable addictions; ugly parodies of community. I could go on. This isn't the first time I have warned you, you know. If you use your freedom this way, you will not inherit God's kingdom. (Galatians 5:19-21 The Message)

*"Bad ideas can be toxic to your legacy!"*

Relationships (especially those sexual in nature) can be the most TOXIC violation of our imaginations! When we have sex with someone, our imaginations are connected to theirs (even if it is just for a short time). We give the person a chance to reshape our futures because we place the possibility that our futures may be together. Even if we only perceive the person as a recurring "sex buddy", we have connected times of our future, and designated our imaginations to repeatedly create a temporal situation of which your time can never be restored. Additionally, your legacy can be affected by this temporal ideology if pregnancy does become the outcome and your legacy has been violated.

When two people come together in sexual intercourse, the process of creation takes place physically and spiritually; the two realms are merged in love. The child that results, is a product of both individuals, and magnetizes spiritually to both.

From when I left the hospital with my son, I knew that it was him and I. My mother was with us, but her flight was set to depart in less than one week, so this left me believing that the responsibility was entirely mine.

His father was still in the process of prioritizing parenthood. He would make statements like, "Should I go out with my friends or should I buy diapers". These statements would let me know that even though at one point, I had perceived unity and marriage potential, the reality was now different. The first four years of his life were extremely

## THE WORLD NEEDS THE GIFT THAT ONLY YOU HAS!

dependent on me, and after I married (when he was four), the responsibilities were shared with my husband. My son would see his father no more than two weeks out of the year, but he always had an interest in getting to know him.

Our family blended gracefully. You would have thought we had been together his entire life because of the love that God had gifted us. Despite our family structure and his father's absence, when my son turned seven and went on summer break from school, I asked him, "What do you want to do during your summer break". He responded, "I want to go to Georgia with my dad". At his request, I had to make it happen. Sending my son away in the summer of 2014 taught me a lot about the power of biology.

Whether both parents stay engaged with the child, greatly dictates the spiritual wellbeing of the child, and effects the legacy of all those to follow that child. Only thru miraculous intervention can the child maintain the spiritual wellness eluding egoic control thoughts of devalue and depreciation. Thankfully, God saw fit to allow my family His redemption power, and His peace. For some that are not yielded, the same bad idea (sex outside of marriage) can cause tremendous pollution to their family line.

## REACH YOUR HIGHEST POTENTIAL!

Your legacy can be affected by the toxicity of the environment of the media, music, and other things that can infiltrate our senses. Stimulate your environment with sound and visual aids that induce the manifestation of your visions! Do as the ants, protect your legacy and your creations!

**"Good ideas can enhance your legacy"**

The Bible tells the story of Ruth, a wealthy girl from Moab, a pagan nation. She married into the family of Elimelech, Naomi, and their two sons. The family that Ruth married into were Jews who were submitted to God. Shortly after her marriage, tragedy set, and Elimilech and his two sons died; leaving Naomi and Ruth as widows.

In sorrow, Naomi chose to leave Moab, and return to her hometown in Jerusalem. Although she would be leaving a prominent lifestyle, family, and the support of loved ones, Ruth opted to return to Jerusalem with her poor mother-in-law.

Over time, Ruth caught the eye of a prominent Jewish man, Boaz, they got married, and from their lineage bore many prominent historic men such as King David, King Solomon, and Jesus.

Naomi could have chosen to pursue her previous

**THE WORLD NEEDS THE GIFT THAT ONLY YOU HAS!**

life style, but a good idea dynamically effected her lineage, and she has become a woman remembered across the globe and the seed bearer to the world's message of love.

**"Bad ideas can be toxic to your talents and your creation"**

You have to free yourself to accept the individual that you are. Your are who you are! You are flawless in your talents, but you must appreciate the individual movement within. You must be open to allowing your art form to evoke new ideas and new emotions from others. You are a new vessel to be used in a different way, manifesting new things from the spiritual realm.

I have always been an artist. From as early as I remember, I loved to draw. It is the only area in life that I had an apparent meticulous trait. I would spend hours drawing one picture, then get frustrated, tear it up, and throw it away. I strived to make my paintings appear to be real, so I would sacrifice the value of an emotion-invoking image for a photographic image.

I am also a dancer. I have explored many different forms; ballet, hip-hop, jazz, character, tap, modern, and many others. I was awarded a full ride scholarship to dance from the Cuyahoga Valley Youth

**REACH YOUR HIGHEST POTENTIAL!**

Ballet at the age of eight and stayed until the fifth grade. I had the opportunity to participate in modeling for the American Girls as Addy walker and perform in many dances. All along, I was one of three African American girls in this ballet company of approximately one hundred dancers enrolled. My parents removed me from the dance company because of the extreme differentiation of standards between the dancer of color and the Caucasian dancers. The company owner, Nan, would speak to the African American dancers very demeaning; she was downright rude. She demanded that we were not to participate in school functions, so that we could be at practice, and my parents eventually got fed up.

They continued to cultivate my desire to dance because they noted that I strived for perfection in it; attempting at making my body mold into the shape and moves of the others around me. In our leotards, it was obvious that I had extra shape in my thighs. When I would point my feet, it was obvious that I had no arch. I loved to dance, but the things that I could not emulate, were saddening to me.

Beginning in the fourth grade, I started to learn how to play the viola. In the sixth grade, I audi-

**THE WORLD NEEDS THE GIFT THAT ONLY YOU HAS!**

tioned to play in the orchestra at the art school (of which I previously gained my position as a visual artist). I had gained skill at the viola. I learned all the chords, played many songs for those who were highly skilled, and I had many opportunities to perform in concert, but I always felt defective because I did not have the innate ability to play by ear.

Over time, I learned that I was projecting my environment on my creation. I was confined to the art forms and the expressions that I had seen before. As an artist, our responsibilities are to communicate a message that evokes transformation; it does not require that the image appears real, that the performance accentuate the most arched foot, or that the melody be played without ever having been written on a Bass or Treble clef. It requires us to look within, examine the cry of the soul, and release the message for the enlightenment of others.

The most paramount thing that you must protect to maintain your creative ability is your imagination. As previously noted, King Solomon said, "There is nothing new under the sun". Our imagination is the spiritual place where we can see the new things, and by your faith, you can bring them to fruition. If your sensory thoughts, emotions, or environment are clouding your thoughts, you stagnate your abil-

## REACH YOUR HIGHEST POTENTIAL!

ities to create.

I learned that the absence of realism in my art is not a flaw. The absence of my arch, flexibility, or peach skin complexion when I dance is not a flaw. I was so focused on the absence of the natural ability to play music, but the music that I did play without notes was not bad. As an artist and creator, I am who I am.

**THE WORLD NEEDS THE GIFT THAT ONLY YOU HAS!**

# PERCEPTION EXERCISE

Write down your ideas from the day, and the effect they would have if you invested your time into them.

**REACH YOUR HIGHEST POTENTIAL!**

# CHAPTER SEVEN: THE POWER OF CREATION

*"Identify Your Strength So That You Can Multiply Your Success"*

Another role of yours is embedded with your talents. Each person is born with talents that they should use to uplift others. For some they may be artists, others are athletic, others are cooks, and on and on. You will know your areas of increased mastery and your talents by paying close attention to the reasons why people initiate conversation with you. Why do you friends call you? Why do you get emails? What are your typical text messages about? These are all clues.

Scientists have observed that soldier ants guard the entrance of an ant colony. They use their heads to plug the entrance, so that they can ensure everyone inside is protected.

Similarly, you must protect your creation. The head is the command center of the body, and the body cannot move without the head. You must protect your creation knowing that it is something you have manifested that no one else can.

## THE WORLD NEEDS THE GIFT THAT ONLY YOU HAS!

Before gaining confidence in my purpose, I would get phone calls where people would request my help with product creation or ideas. Some people would call and ask me to pray with them. Others were calling me to ask me if what they wrote or what they said sounded good. All these calls and messages were not a light bulb on that my purpose was out singing the tune of my current job either in McDonald's or as a Public Health Technician in the military. People were not calling me for my taught expertise, but for my natural innate abilities and passions. My passion gave me determination to find specified knowledge, but it all connected to my purpose. What is that for you?

Your creation is also vitally important! The things that you use your talents and abilities to portray are as distinguished as your fingerprints; they cannot be replicated or replaced. You are the only one that can create what you have created, and the things that you create are manifested as your ministry to others; they can evoke emotion and change simply by contact. You should hold value and esteem to the things that you create. In the face of threats such as environmental dishonesty (hatred, robbery, burglary, or destruction), you should move your creations, so that their ministry can continue.

**REACH YOUR HIGHEST POTENTIAL!**

Jesus said, "Man does not live from bread and water alone, but every word that proceeds from the mouth of the Father". Accordingly, He told us that food, water, and words are our subsistence. The Father spoke words of creation. When we receive words of creation (ideas that uplift our purpose, encouragement, prophecy, etc.), we must protect those words. The Bible tells us that our opposition is not flesh and blood, the Course in Miracles tells us that our opposition is our ego, and the Tao Te Ching tells us that our opposition is fear; all of these texts reinforce that we have the power to overcome ALL things that we perceive as opposition. When we perceive opposition dressed in a garment of our ego exalting attributes of individualism and self-esteem, we have to protect our subsistence and flee! In an environment of fear and doubt, we do not have to share the words of prophecy that we were given, but instead, we should protect them!

As an artist in the military, I experienced many times where I would have the urge to draw or to write, but I had a work-related assignment or a self-assigned motherly duty that I allowed to restrain me from accomplishing this task. I did not realize how to monetize my abilities or how to market my skills well enough to make an impact on the lives of others. My talents seemed to be just "for fun". Accord-

**THE WORLD NEEDS THE GIFT THAT ONLY YOU HAS!**

ingly, I would overlook the importance of creating.

As I gained wisdom, I learned how distinguished my talents were, and I was able to witness the impact that I made when I would use my talents. When I would dance, people would express the emotional release that they had experienced thru my art. When I painted, I would see the joy that I could gift to someone as they looked upon my artwork and gained understanding of its message. In writing, my reviews, phone calls, and messages would relay how my blog or my books had made an impact in the lives of others. The feedback that I get is so refreshing that it is a continuous reminder of the purpose and the value that I offer others. I learned that my daily bread is much more than I had ever imagined.

My daily bread is the smile on the faces of others who are the recipients of me just being. You don't usually recognize the spiritual commerce as it is taking place, but as you are walking about, others are observing. They are attentive to what you wear, how you talk, how you smell, your posture, and many other facets of your being. You can encourage or discourage just in being; without intention. Do you encourage others to walk in diligence? Do they speak honorably because they heard you?

When our being can make someone else smile, can

**REACH YOUR HIGHEST POTENTIAL!**

encourage someone to connect to their purpose, increase the love that a person experiences in their life, or improves another person's quality of life, it is our daily bread. When we have blessed a person in our being, we may be met with a smile, a sigh, a laugh, a hug, or another form or expression of exhilaration; this is our daily bread. Your daily bread is also any other form of subsistence to include food, shelter, clothing, oxygen, confidence, and love. You must protect them all! In her book, Why it Matters, and What You Can Do To Get More Of It, Kelly McGonigal says, "The biggest enemies of willpower: temptation, self-criticism, and stress. (...) these three skills, self-awareness, self-care, and remembering what matter most are the foundation for self-control."

**THE WORLD NEEDS THE GIFT THAT ONLY YOU HAS!**

# PERCEPTION EXERCISE

1. What have you created?

|   |
|---|
|   |
|   |
|   |
|   |

2. What can you create?

|   |
|---|
|   |
|   |
|   |
|   |

3. What are ways that you can use your creations to serve others?

|   |
|---|
|   |
|   |
|   |
|   |

**REACH YOUR HIGHEST POTENTIAL!**

# CHAPTER EIGHT: THE POWER OF PROPERTY

Your energy is raised by thanksgiving. Gratitude changes the momentum of negative thoughts, and breaks self-hindering walls that you have built (knowingly or unknowingly). Property is the most common idle known to man. Anything that man can consider "mine", can easily be re-altered in the mind, and take precedence before the reverence of God. The problem with ownership is that it is not the truth. Man is only the ambassador of the Earth's property; not the owner. Man has access rather than ownership.

When the concept of access to property rather than the ownership is grasped, you can be relieved knowing that the owner is responsible for the maintenance and subsistence of creation; not you.

Similar to a tenant and a landlord, if you own the property, you are responsible for the upkeep, maintenance, taxes, etc. The tenant has access to the property, but no major obligation to ensure upkeep.

Property is your dominion (in your authority not ownership) and can be contributory to your pur-

**THE WORLD NEEDS THE GIFT THAT ONLY YOU HAS!**

pose. It is not an entitlement; it can be given and taken away at any moment. Property should not be misused as a source of validation or symbol of something that only the Spirit can grant such as freedom, value, prestige, character, etc. Many get access to money and feel the need to buy bigger, more features, and more flash to expose that they have been gifted. When we are submitted to Pride and Lust, we can easily alter the use of good property.

When you step on an ant colony, they immediately respond in defense. They head towards whatever is causing danger to their colony regardless of its size. They understand that their property is a tool for the manifestation of their purpose. Within their colony is their eggs, their egg-laying queen, their young, and their food.

Property should be a tool to promote your purpose, not a hindrance or interference, but it is your responsibility to value it appropriately, and maintain dominion over it rather than allowing property to own you.

We should not uphold the definition of physical things assigned by another, but rather assign one ourselves. Very often, in the physical world, goods

**REACH YOUR HIGHEST POTENTIAL!**

can be displayed and universal pricing placed on each object. In most instances, value is projected by the producer and other consumers. Our interests can be inflated just by others' agreement of high value. This should not happen! We should not change our interests because a high value has been assigned to something, but rather we should analyze each thing, and place its value based upon its importance to our life purpose.

Your story, talents, body, ideas, creation, and property are all powerful tools that you can use to execute your purpose. Adversely, they can also be misused. These tools are all within your dominion on the Earth, and should not hold dominion over you. You should never be controlled by the thoughts that your story; your past or otherwise, is in control because you have dominion over it. You should never be controlled by ideas that you can't do something because your car, your house, your animal, etc., is a hinderance because you have dominion. You should never be controlled by ideas that you can't do something because your body, or your not smart enough, not talented enough, not creative enough because God instilled everything that you need for your assignment in you. Your responsibility is to value what you have by making use of it.

**THE WORLD NEEDS THE GIFT THAT ONLY YOU HAS!**

# PERCEPTION EXERCISE

1. What do you have to be gratful for? Write ten things below:

|   |
|---|
|   |
|   |
|   |
|   |

2. Is there anything that you own that has taken posesion of you? Is there anything that you are trying to keep that prevents you from pursuing your purpose?

|   |
|---|
|   |
|   |
|   |
|   |

3. How can you ensure that you maintain dominion over your proerty rather than it ruling you?

|   |
|---|
|   |
|   |
|   |
|   |

4. How can you use your property to advance your life

**REACH YOUR HIGHEST POTENTIAL!**

purpose?

**THE WORLD NEEDS THE GIFT THAT ONLY YOU HAS!**

# CHAPTER NINE: THE POWER OF FAITH

Potential means what could be. What could be if you were not worried about funds, who will watch your kids, if you had not been afraid, if you weren't worried about what he/she said, or had not said, "never mind". Your potential is an abundance of possibilities. Dr. Myles Munroe says that most people are only utilizing 10% of their potential, while 90% lies dormant. When you stare at your vision board, with no doubts or fears in mind (above your thoughts, not succumb to them), what steps can you actively take now to pursue that vision?

We all have a step that we can take towards that vision that we see, what is yours? There are powers that we all have that despite how sizeable our visions may be, we can exercise our powers to successfully execute.

Insects.about.com says:

"Ants are capable of carrying objects 50 times their own body weight with their mandibles.

## REACH YOUR HIGHEST POTENTIAL!

Ants use their diminutive size to their advantage. Relative to their size, their muscles are thicker than those of larger animals or even humans. This ratio enables them to produce more force and carry larger objects. If we had muscles in the proportions of ants, we'd be able to heave a Hyundai over our heads!"

Humans also have great potential to carry into physicality much more than they assign themselves to when they apply their faith. Faith is the spiritual muscles that we use to pull spiritual things into physical existence. Faith is not a spirit as wisdom, but it is a substance. Faith has never been personified as speaking to us as wisdom, fear, or folly. Faith is a substance like glue.

I am an American citizen. As an American citizen, I can receive welfare benefits, tax benefits, healthcare benefits, and access to areas of the Earth as a result in my belief in the citizenship rights. If I do not believe in my citizenship rights (even in regards to the moral quality of them), I would not apply or be receptive of the access that I have. Additionally, I have signage that I am an American citizen (my birth certificate, my ID, my passport, my vehicle registration, and so on).

**THE WORLD NEEDS THE GIFT THAT ONLY YOU HAS!**

Similarly, as Kingdom citizens, we have access to heavenly benefits. We receive healthcare benefits, welfare benefits, we have taxation, we have laws, we have military support to defend us, we have property, we have responsibilities, and we have a King.

Faith is the currency required to make heavenly purchases manifest on the Earth. Without faith, you will not have manifestation.

**REACH YOUR HIGHEST POTENTIAL!**

### PERCEPTION EXERCISE

This poem is a faith affirmation. I want you to read it with zeal and excitement!

# I AM LIKE AN ANT

I am like an ant
I work with a team
I know how to live among others
I leave others signals to advance.
I have a team that follow me to fruition
I know how to live in abundance
No one on my team worries about lack
I do not rely on anyone else for my provisions
God alone provides for me
I do not rely on anyone else for my direction
God alone directs me
I gather in harvest
I am prepared all year long
Until death do I part from God's plan for me
I fight for my life
I fight for my dreams
I fight for my visions
I fight for my team
I do not disperse because of obstacles
I gather my team and concur opposition
To some, I may be small, but I am still more

Tiffany Domena

## THE WORLD NEEDS THE GIFT THAT ONLY YOU HAS!

powerful than those who are large.
I can carry many times my weight
I have multiplied myself to be more abundant than all living things

I am like the ant!

**REACH YOUR HIGHEST POTENTIAL!**

# CHAPTER TEN: THE POWER OF SUBMISSION

If you demonstrate the love to others in your desire to love so much that you abandon your "self", and follow the footsteps that were placed into our imaginations as a possibility by Jesus, this is the power of the blood of the Lamb. Sacrifice yourself for love. Crucify your doubts, fears, lusts, greed, and all other hindrances for the sake of the impact that you can have in the life of another. Affect volumes! Paul says:

I appeal to you therefore, brethren, *and* beg of you in view of [all] the mercies of God, to make a decisive dedication of your bodies [presenting all your members and faculties] as a living sacrifice, holy (devoted, consecrated) and well pleasing to God, which is your reasonable (rational, intelligent) service *and* spiritual worship.

Do not be conformed to this world (this age), [fashioned after and adapted to its external, superficial customs], but be transformed (changed) by the [entire] renewal of your mind

**THE WORLD NEEDS THE GIFT THAT ONLY YOU HAS!**

[by its new ideals and its new attitude], so that you may prove [for yourselves] what is the good and acceptable and perfect will of God, *even* the thing which is good and acceptable and perfect [in His sight for you].

`For by the grace (unmerited favor of God) given to me I warn everyone among you not to estimate *and* think of himself more highly than he ought [not to have an exaggerated opinion of his own importance], but to rate his ability with sober judgment, each according to the degree of faith apportioned by God to him.

The ants do not have the ego. They do not ponder whether self-identity is more important than corporate purpose. They are continually submitted to the colony purpose, which is how they work in unity without a ruler, commander, or overseer.

Submission to the Kingdom is the time when we have removed sovereignty from all influences, and have pointed our openness to our King. God spoke to King David saying, "He says, "Be still, and know that I am God; I will be exalted among the nations, I will be exalted in the earth."(Psalms 46:10) In our time of stillness, we can exert the patience necessary to gain the

## REACH YOUR HIGHEST POTENTIAL!

wisdom or knowledge required to fulfill our purpose.

The Bible says in Hosea 4:8, "My people are destroyed for lack of knowledge; because you [the priestly nation] have rejected knowledge, I will also reject you that you shall be no priest to Me; seeing you have forgotten the law of your God, I will also forget your children. The Bible says that fail because of lack of knowledge. Being receptive of wisdom is your greatest self-inflicted limitation, but with God all things are possible."
"When we are in submission to God, we can expect miracles to continuously manifest."

Our perceptions are based solely on the past, and the past does not govern the present or the future. We choose to base our future perception based upon the past, but God did not create that way; this is called projection. God created.

Creation is the process of forming something entirely new; something unperceived before. Every second is a part of creation, and because we are made in the image of God, we have the opportunity to participate in the creation of the future rather than to expect the future because

## THE WORLD NEEDS THE GIFT THAT ONLY YOU HAS!

of the patterns of the past. Our participation in creation is dependent on our level of submission; submission to using good ideas, to love, and to service. When we are submitted, we can expect miracles.

So what, many people have died of this disease before! So what, many people have tried overcoming this obstacle before! So what, your parents and grandparents were like this! Creation is happening now. Miracles are those things that defy the pattern of the past, and you can expect them when you are submitted to God. Expect miracles. Expect that the collections of energy that have formed to make your environment would diffuse for the good of those that you have been assigned to bless.

Moses was an Israelite man, spoken of in the book of Exodus of the Bible. He was favored by God as a baby, and therefore saved from the universal annihilation that was happening to the remainder of the Jewish babies. Even more profound, he was raised in the castle of the king who disseminated the order to kill all of the Jewish babies. When Moses grew up, he had a face to face encounter with the Spirit of God thru a burning bush, and there God revealed to him his purpose for his life-to free the Israelites from enslavement. Over the course of years, Moses manifest many miraculous feats which express that

## REACH YOUR HIGHEST POTENTIAL!

the culmination of energy that we see and call it a lake, a sea, a mountain, a tree, or whatever we have defined it, by no means is required to maintain its form if we decree it otherwise. The universe conformed to the salvation of the Israelites; the red sea split into two so they could walk down the middle, the sky rained food, their clothes maintained their form for 40+ years, and many more requests were yielded to show us that our pre-assumed diagnosis of earthly expectation based upon the past has no value because creation is constantly taking place.

Moses did not have power of his own. He stayed submitted to the voice of God.

Everything physical is perceived as a pattern because it has been assigned a rhythm by God, however, He can change it. Everything has been created to reveal His attributes; He does not change. He has made the Earth where we can perceive that it does not change, however it does but, it has its place in His eternal message.

**THE WORLD NEEDS THE GIFT THAT ONLY YOU HAS!**

## PERCEPTION EXERCISE

Take three to four periods 30-min periods throughout the day to be still. Remove your mind from your emotions, feelings, thoughts, and just be still. Announce before, "Speak Lord, your servnnt is listening", and just be still. Be okay with however God responds, but practice remaining open to His voice. This may feel uncomforatble, and at times, you may convince yourself that it is worthless, God sees you, and values time with you.

# CHAPTER ELEVEN: THE POWER OF FORGIVENESS

The entire physical world is a plethora of very minute bodies of energy, which have been collected for our perception thru channels that God has made for us: body, eyes, ears, nose, and mouth. We assume that just because the energy has been collected and perceived by us in one way that it is the universal perception, but this is not true. Every person receives a different message thru their channels of perception. What I see is different than what you see, what I hear is different than what you hear, what you feel is different than what I feel, and so on. No two people perceive things exactly the same, and because we become accustom to believing that perceptions are the same, relationships become very unstable. Understanding is yielding to another's perception. Forgiveness is assigning the ego to his rightful place, and yielding to the Spirit of love.

Matthew 6:14-15, "For if you forgive people their trespasses [their reckless and willful sins, leaving them, letting them go, and giving up resentment], your heavenly Father will also forgive you.

**THE WORLD NEEDS THE GIFT THAT ONLY YOU HAS!**

But if you do not forgive others their trespasses [their reckless and willful sins, leaving them, letting them go, and giving up resentment], neither will your Father forgive you your trespasses.

Forgiveness has the ability to open the gates of heaven and Earth or close them. If you harbor unforgiveness, you close heaven and Earth's gate. As Dr. Myles Munroe said, and is biblically supported, "Forgiveness is a key to Kingdom access."

The ants don't hesitate to act on matters. When the ant colony is on fire, in a hurricane or tornado, or whatever the situation; they choose their route, and they go.

When we harbor unforgiveness, it causes us to reroute because we do not want to talk about certain matters, we may not want to see the person, we may not even want to be in the same location. In essence, the unforgiveness causes us to act and think differently.

We are reflections of love, which is omnipresent. When we harbor unforgiveness, we are self-containing ourselves to inhibit the flow of love to our neighbor. The truth of it is that even with our great-

## REACH YOUR HIGHEST POTENTIAL!

est effort, love cannot be limited, and will flow even with the presence of unforgiveness. Unforgiveness is a miscreation of our own perception that results in health ailments for the person that harbors it. The body is the classroom for the mind to practice creation. When we create walls of resistance between our brothers and sisters, they manifest in our own being.

If you wanted to eat, your fork and your hand could be the substances that you use to escort the food into your mouth. If you want to manifest your visions for your life, faith must be the substance that you use to grab things from the spiritual realm to the physical realm. Faith is your spiritual limbs. Love creates everything that you request in the spiritual realm, but you have to be strong enough and knowledgeable enough to grab what is yours. It is not the "devil" that is impeding you from manifesting. For the most part, it is ignorance of how to use your spiritual limbs. Get comfortable with using your spiritual limbs! Make them very strong because they will do much more for you than anything physical. In fact, nothing physical will be possible without your spiritual limbs.

**THE WORLD NEEDS THE GIFT THAT ONLY YOU HAS!**

## PERCEPTION EXERCISE

Think of a person that you have not yet forgiven. Allow the feelings that you feel towards that person to roam thru your mind. Do not run from your emotion, but face it. This person may be dead or alive; accessible or inaccessible. Write a letter of forgiveness to this person. Free yourself from the bondage of stagnating your future! You do not have to give it to them, but write this letter to free yourself.

|   |
|---|
|   |
|   |
|   |
|   |
|   |
|   |
|   |
|   |
|   |
|   |
|   |
|   |
|   |
|   |

**REACH YOUR HIGHEST POTENTIAL!**

# CHAPTER TWELVE: THE POWER OF DILIGENCE

Do not hold onto a "have it all now" attitude! It is so common for us to believe that because we see something (physically or spiritually), we should have it now. Peter said in 2 Peter 1:4-6:

By means of these He has bestowed on us His precious and exceedingly great promises, so that through them you may escape [by flight] from the moral decay (rottenness and corruption) that is in the world because of covetousness (lust and greed), and become sharers (partakers) of the divine nature. For this very reason, adding your diligence [to the divine promises], employ every effort in exercising your faith to develop virtue (excellence, resolution, Christian energy), and in [exercising] virtue [develop] knowledge (intelligence), And in [exercising] knowledge [develop] self-control, and in [exercising] self-control [develop] steadfastness (patience, endurance), and in [exercising] steadfastness [develop] godliness (piety).

## REACH YOUR HIGHEST POTENTIAL!

I saw the ants demonstrate diligence when a bear was digging in soil. Over the course of his digging, he found himself with paws covered with ants. The colony continued to pour out with ants going towards the bear, and crawling all over him. Humorously, the bear began doing this shaking and "get off of me" dance, but to no avail. The ants were determined to defend their colony, headed towards him, and did not stop targeting him until he ran off.

Despite the ant's size, they were not deterred from the bear. Though not all of them were in danger, their priority was to break the bear's will to demolish their colony, so they headed towards him. Even at 1000+ times greater than their size, the bear still did not win the battle against the ants.

Rather than staring at the size of your bear, ask yourself, "Is his will stronger than mine?" Your bear may be your laziness. Maybe you desire to just be home and relax. You don't want to get up and do what is necessary for success. Ask yourself, "Is the will of that bear stronger than mine?" You may be experiencing opposition in relationships where people are against your necessities for success. Ask yourself, "Is the bears' will stronger than mine?". You are as capable as the ant to overturn your situation if you exercise the same mentality that they did. They ran towards the attack with full force and confidence.

**THE WORLD NEEDS THE GIFT THAT ONLY YOU HAS!**

The ants exercise diligence; diligence in gathering their food, diligence in travel, and diligence in everything that they do. Diligence is the power that you use when you are submitted to manifesting something of God.

You must have a strong enough desire to bring forth that you are willing to conquer the opposition that comes up. When your self-control is wavering, diligence says, "Stay on course". When tragedy happens, diligence says, "I still have to push". When your schedule is sporadic, diligence says, "I have to set time aside for this".

God exercises diligence in His creation. Even at that point, He allowed the process to maintain. He allowed the process of man giving birth to generations, rather than populating Earth at the beginning. He allowed the process of seeds being planted into the ground, and growing into a plant, rather than filling the Earth with forestry enough to sustain generations.

He bestowed power in the process. It is the process that strengthens the testimony. I remember when I decided to alleviate my hair of the chemicals that I had been using to burn it for years. By nature, my hair has numerous tight pencil-like coils. As

## REACH YOUR HIGHEST POTENTIAL!

a result of a fad that I had been watching, I chose to straighten my hair with chemicals in the eighth grade. It took several processing treatments to get the ends of my hair completely obedient to the chemical treatment that I had allowed the beautician to place in there.

After years of running my fingers over my extremely beveled scalp (full of scars and scabs), I decided to abandon the chemicals, but it wasn't that easy. Getting rid of the chemicals was also a process. I had to cut all of the processed hair off, and regrow my natural curl pattern. Throughout the process of regrowing my hair, I learned how to maintain this new texture that I had grown completely unfamiliar with. I had to use new hair are products, new combs and brushes, and so on.

Your journey to the fulfillment of your purpose is a process. You will be embracing new textures, and new depths of your reality. Just as I had to re-learn how to comb my hair, you will also have to discern how to interact with those divine participants in your life's journey, how to be open to the portals that bring the funding for your life's purpose, and so on. Diligence is the practice of consistently acting on a formula for production. The book of wisdom says:

## THE WORLD NEEDS THE GIFT THAT ONLY YOU HAS!

- He becomes poor who works with a slack *and* idle hand, but the hand of the diligent makes rich. (Proverbs 10:4)

- He who diligently seeks good seeks [God's] favor, but he who searches after evil, it shall come upon him. (Proverbs 11:27)

- The slothful man does not catch his game *or* roast it once he kills it, but the diligent man gets precious possessions. (Proverbs 12:27)

- The thoughts of the [steadily] diligent tend only to plenteousness, but everyone who is impatient *and* hasty hastens only to want. (Proverbs 21:5)

- Do you see a man diligent *and* skillful in his business? He will stand before kings; he will not stand before obscure men. (Proverbs 22:29)

Additionally, you cannot have the quitter attitude either. Regardless of your definition of success, it never comes easy. It is a natural part of being a physical being. We were born into the world that had been cursed as a result of Adam. When we are ready to quit, remember the ant. He fights until death.

Even when a single ant is dropped into water, he

**REACH YOUR HIGHEST POTENTIAL!**

kicks until he can't kick anymore. When an ant is injured, his legs still remain kicking, his antennas are still moving. He stays in motion until death.

When we connect to the Spirit, we can connect to the fruits. It is possible for us to experience the ease, the freedom, and the love of Heaven. For this reason, Jesus said that we should pray that the Kingdom of Heaven come on Earth. It is possible for Heaven to manifest on Earth, but it only does so at our request. Apostle Paul says:

But the fruit of the [Holy] Spirit [the work which His presence within accomplishes] is love, joy (gladness), peace, patience (an even temper, forbearance), kindness, goodness (benevolence), faithfulness, Gentleness (meekness, humility), self-control (self-restraint, continence). Against such things there is no law [that can bring a charge]. (Galatians 5:55-23)
"Diligence does not have to be painful."

When Jesus died, He broke the covenant that man had established with Satan in the Garden of Eden. He took the keys back and returned our inheritance to us. From this point on, we were restored as Kingdom ambassadors of Heaven. The Father acknowledges our role so much that He honors our will. If

## THE WORLD NEEDS THE GIFT THAT ONLY YOU HAS!

we invite Him, He will give us rest, freedom, health, and all other benefits of Kingdom citizenship. If we do not invite Him, and choose to be primarily submitted to Earthly authority, we have to bear the toil and heartache that is a result of permitting this authority over us. Jesus said:

"The Father has given me all these things to do and say. This is a unique Father-Son operation, coming out of Father and Son intimacies and knowledge. No one knows the Son the way the Father does, nor the Father the way the Son does. But I'm not keeping it to myself; I'm ready to go over it line by line with anyone willing to listen.

"Are you tired? Worn out? Burned out on religion? Come to me. Get away with me and you'll recover your life. I'll show you how to take a real rest. Walk with me and work with me—watch how I do it. Learn the unforced rhythms of grace. I won't lay anything heavy or ill-fitting on you. Keep company with me and you'll learn to live freely and lightly." Because our minds are so easily focused on the physical world, and doing things the physical way, we lose the connection, the grace, and take on our own yolk. (Matthew 11:27-30)

Without the Spirit, diligence is painful. With the

**REACH YOUR HIGHEST POTENTIAL!**

Spirit of God, diligence can be a delight, and you can see the fruit of your labor.

**THE WORLD NEEDS THE GIFT THAT ONLY YOU HAS!**

# PERCEPTION EXERCISE

Write down 10 ways that you can exercise more diligence in your daily life.

|   |
|---|
|   |
|   |
|   |
|   |
|   |
|   |
|   |
|   |
|   |
|   |
|   |
|   |
|   |
|   |
|   |
|   |
|   |
|   |
|   |
|   |

Perception: The World's Most Affluent Leader

**REACH YOUR HIGHEST POTENTIAL!**

# CHAPTER THIRTEEN: THE POWER OF VOLUME

The difference in the successful and the unsuccessful lies greatly in the depths that they go to be of service to others. Successful people must forsake their doubts, their ideas of "maybe they will say this or that about me", and all of their other fears. They have to free themselves to the ideas that "I am valuable to everyone", "my service is worth paying for", "My service is a result of a heavenly outpour", and "my service is a part of my daily bread".

The ant is not known much for auditory volume. However, the ant clearly demonstrates the power of numbers and collaboration; each ant submitted to his assignment within the colony. Scientists say that the total biomass of all the ants on Earth is roughly equal to the total biomass of all the people on Earth. Ants have been observed using their large numbers as an advantage to overcome large beings, natural disasters, and many other obstacles that have caused the demise of beings much larger than they.

Volume is intensity, audibility, loudness, mass, or

## THE WORLD NEEDS THE GIFT THAT ONLY YOU HAS!

quantity. In whichever context, volume is powerful!

Auditory volume has the ability to transform body functions by the intensity of its vibration. Intense vibration has been tested to be a healing agent for varying skeletal disorders. Volume also has an affect on the brain system. Certain intensities of sound can subliminally reprogram the brain. If you diligently engage the brain with empowering audio, you can transform the hindering and self-impeding beliefs (I will speak more on this later).

Volume in regards to quantity is extremely powerful. In accordance with Pareto's law, economists say that 80% of results come from 20% of actions. Otherwise said, 80% of responses come from 20% of people. How big is your 100%? How many people do you know? How many people have you made yourself (or your purpose) known to? If this number is small, this could be a key to why you are not manifesting large results. Utilize the power of diligence to leverage your visibility and make known to the world the unique purpose that God has bestowed on you!

Surround yourself with clusters of people who are aspiring to reach their highest potential. There is power in groups and numbers. One drop of rain ab-

**REACH YOUR HIGHEST POTENTIAL!**

sorbs quickly, but several can create traumatic impact.

**THE WORLD NEEDS THE GIFT THAT ONLY YOU HAS!**

# PERCEPTION EXERCISE

1. What type of people would benefit your purpose? What are their careers? What is their charater like? What are their passions? What is your mission with them?

Perception: The World's Most Affluent Leader

**REACH YOUR HIGHEST POTENTIAL!**

# CHAPTER FOURTEEN: THE POWER OF THE WORD

The Spirit does not see the lack and the malfunction that the ego sees. The Spirit is confident that there is always a solution, and when we submit to this, we can be aligned. From nothing, God used the word to create. The phrase in Hebrew is נִשְׁמַת חַיִּים (*nishmat chayyim*). The Hebrew word typically translated as "spirit" in English is רוּחַ (*ruach*). The article Mysticism of the Sound says that breath could also be translated as word. John says that in the beginning was the Word, then later in the book tells us that Jesus is the Word. Jesus told us that He is breath, life, truth, and light. When man was created, breath was given to him, and this allowed him to demonstrate the abilities of which we now associate with life.

For the ant, the words are chemicals called pheromone. The pheromone is used to communicate where others can find food, be relieved of threat, advance to their colony, and so on. Words, whether discovered thru chemical translation or auditory fulfill the purpose of creation, unity, and love; they are another form of connection between one being

## THE WORLD NEEDS THE GIFT THAT ONLY YOU HAS!

and another.

Each human inhales 34,560 times per day if they breath once every 2.5 seconds which tells us that we are given breath/life multiple times per day. Our bodies have been instilled with the ability to identify oxygen as a receptacle of our nutrients, and we inhale it using our autonomic brain system. For most, we do not even have to intend to breath to perform the breath. You do not understand the depth of gratitude that you should have for God's continual choice to give you life.

The word created the universe and everything that we see, the breath sustains life, and the vibration sustains the form of everything that we see. Without the continual rhythm of our hearts, we would be dead, and our flesh would begin the process of deterioration.

Just as God by the Word or breath began the vibration that formed the world, you also have the ability to create or destruct by your words. Saying, "I can't" is a toxic word because in it, you call God a liar, and face rebuke as a result. Saying "I am" weak, poor, worn out, unable, or so on, is a confession of separation from God.

## REACH YOUR HIGHEST POTENTIAL!

In a vibrational sense, your words cause a shift of form with each breath. If you observe your living arrangement today, and live for 100 years without changing anything, the place would still change.

In a spiritual collaborative sense, you have impact with your words because in them, you have the ability to encourage or discourage. We are formless in our essence. God confessed to being formless when Moses asked him, "Who do I say sent me?", and He replied, "I am that, I am". His confession was that everything that you see is me. When you see the sky, "I am that", when you see the water, "I am that". Since we are created in His image, and connected to Him, having dominion over the Earth and rights in Heaven, we also have abilities in the likeness of God. At no point should we defy the truth of who we are even if we have separated from God spiritually, and therefore are manifesting a likeness alternative to the abundance that God declares.

**THE WORLD NEEDS THE GIFT THAT ONLY YOU HAS!**

# PERCEPTION EXERCISE

Write down 10 positive "I AM" affirmations.

# CHAPTER FIFTEEN: THE POWER OF THE BLOOD

Revelations 12:10-11 says:

" Then I heard a strong (loud) voice in heaven, saying, Now it has come—the salvation and the power and the kingdom (the dominion, the reign) of our God, and the power (the sovereignty, the authority) of His Christ (the Messiah); for the accuser of our brethren, he who keeps bringing before our God charges against them day and night, has been cast out! And they have overcome (conquered) him by means of the blood of the Lamb and by the utterance of their testimony, for they did not love *and* cling to life even when faced with death [holding their lives cheap till they had to die for their witnessing]."

What is the blood of the Lamb and why is so much emphasis placed on it? I was raised in church and I have heard on countless times, "I place the blood of the lamb from the top of his/her head to the soles of his/her feet!", but what does that mean? There are many songs written on the blood. One song says, "The blood that gives me strength from day to

**THE WORLD NEEDS THE GIFT THAT ONLY YOU HAS!**

day….It will never lose it's power". How does blood that is unapparent give someone daily power? If the power were in the physical blood, why would God not place the zeal into the hearts of some to make them feel inclined to preserve the literal blood that poured from the body of Jesus? Blood is referenced 392 times in the New International Version of the Bible, but what is the significance, and what does that have to do with you? These questions and more were questions that I asked myself as I explored the power in the blood.

After the fall, the first thing that man did to cover his shame was to sacrifice an animal to use his skin as a covering. Man created the process of covering shame with blood and death. As a result of this life being taken to atone for their guilt, sacrifices were continually offered as a means of atoning for sin. God spoke to the Israelites in Leviticus 17:11 saying, "For the life of a creature is in the blood, and I have given it to you to make atonement for yourselves on the altar; it is the blood that makes atonement for one's life."

It was no mystery to God that man could fall short. God has His plan for the entire world. As He says, "For I know the plans I have for you," declares the LORD, "Plans to prosper you and not to harm you,

**REACH YOUR HIGHEST POTENTIAL!**

plans to give you hope and a future". God has His will, but since He has created us in His image, He has given us our own will too. To those that believe that their deeds do not cunt because God controls them as puppets, God said this to this Israelites in exile with Nebuchadnezzar, "For they have not listened to my words," declares the LORD, "Words that I sent to them again and again by my servants the prophets. And you exiles have not listened either," declares the Lord". We are not puppets! We are freewill beings bestowed with the abilities to create and make choices in the likeness of our Father. We have been sent here as Kingdom Ambassadors of the Kingdom of Heaven. God planned the "if's" and the "then's". He has an outcome to redeem our shortfalls, and He says that despite our shortfalls, "We are assured *and* know that [God being a partner in their labor] all things work together *and* are [fitting into a plan] for good to *and* for those who love God and are called according to [His] design *and* purpose". (Romans 8:28)

God knew the beginning, end, and all of the in-between possibilities of the Earth, which is why he said, "I make known the end from the beginning, from ancient times, what is still to come. I say, 'My purpose will stand, and I will do all that I please."

**THE WORLD NEEDS THE GIFT THAT ONLY YOU HAS!**

The Old Testament of the Bible describes the process where the Israelites would choose animals to sacrifice for certain occasions as a means of redemption. In Exodus 20:24, God says:

An altar of earth you shall make to Me and sacrifice on it your burnt offerings and your peace offerings, your sheep and your oxen. In every place where I record My name and cause it to be remembered I will come to you and bless you.

And in Exodus 12:2-14, He says:

This month shall be to you the beginning of months, the first month of the year to you. Tell all the congregation of Israel, On the tenth day of this month they shall take every man a lamb *or* kid, according to [the size of] the family of which he is the father, a lamb *or* kid for each house. And if the household is too small to consume the lamb, let him and his next door neighbor take it according to the number of persons, every man according to what each can eat shall make your count for the lamb. Your lamb *or* kid shall be without blemish, a male of the first year; you shall take it from the sheep or the goats. And you shall keep it until the fourteenth day of the same month; and the whole assembly of the

**REACH YOUR HIGHEST POTENTIAL!**

congregation of Israel shall [each] kill [his] lamb in the evening. They shall take of the blood and put it on the two side posts and on the lintel [above the door space] of the houses in which they shall eat [the Passover lamb]. They shall eat the flesh that night roasted; with unleavened bread and bitter herbs they shall eat it. Eat not of it raw nor boiled at all with water, but roasted—its head, its legs, and its inner parts. You shall let nothing of the meat remain until the morning; and the bones *and* unedible bits which remain of it until morning you shall burn with fire. And you shall eat it thus: [as fully prepared for a journey] your loins girded, your shoes on your feet, and your staff in your hand; and you shall eat it in haste. It is the Lord's Passover. For I will pass through the land of Egypt this night and will smite all the firstborn in the land of Egypt, both man and beast; and against all the gods of Egypt I will execute judgment [proving their helplessness]. I am the Lord. The blood shall be for a token *or* sign to you upon [the doorposts of] the houses where you are, [that] when I see the blood, I will pass over you, and no plague shall be upon you to destroy you when I smite the land of Egypt. And this day shall be to you for a memorial. You shall keep it as a feast to the Lord throughout your generations, keep it as an ordinance forever.

**THE WORLD NEEDS THE GIFT THAT ONLY YOU HAS!**

Two thousand years later, On the evening of the Passover celebration (a customary time to sacrifice a lamb), Jesus died on the cross. He was a sizeable enough sacrifice to redeem the entire world. In response, Paul said, "For God has done what the Law could not do, [its power] being weakened by the flesh [the entire nature of man without the Holy Spirit]. Sending His own Son in the guise of sinful flesh and as an offering for sin, [God] condemned sin in the flesh [subdued, overcame, deprived it of its power over all who accept that sacrifice]."

Jesus as the redemption lamb for our sin was not a sporadic decision; it was known from the beginning. God knew the possibility that we would fall short. He knows that it is possible for you to have blemishes, and in fact, He knows that we all have blemished because His word says so, but the blood is the symbol of His love for you. It is a symbol of a life that was here on the Earth, but chose nails to be hammered thru his flesh to return to you your inheritance.

The ants will die to defend their colony. The Bible says "Greater love hath no man than this, that a man lay down his life for his friends. (John 15:13) Jesus demonstrated this sacrifice; facing death for the world, and the ants understand the colony holds

**REACH YOUR HIGHEST POTENTIAL!**

higher importance than individual life.

Blood is a symbol of life. Without the circulation of our blood, we die. Blood is also a symbol of love. It is a character that we share with all living beings. Every race shares the same origins when traced by blood, and the concentration of it is tailor-made for our survival. The loss of large quantities of blood causes either our cessation or our freedom to be complete in Spirit. Jesus' choice to loose His life to overcome death, take the keys, and return your inheritance to you is a symbol of the love of God.

**THE WORLD NEEDS THE GIFT THAT ONLY YOU HAS!**

## PERCEPTION EXERCISE

What are you ashamed of? What have you bound deep within because of fear of others' responses. Write the thoughts below and your response after each shameful occurence, "I release myself by the Blood of the Lamb. This will now my destiny".

**REACH YOUR HIGHEST POTENTIAL!**

**THE WORLD NEEDS THE GIFT THAT ONLY YOU HAS!**

# ABOUT THE AUTHOR

Tiffany Domena is a visionary, author, investor, minister, artist, podcaster, marketer, and speaker who is helping others to reach their highest potential in life. She is the author of *Someone Covets You, I Want To Have Impact, But Who Should Be My Mentor?, I Want To Get My Christian Life Together, But Where Do I Start?*, and coming soon, she will be launching, *Transforming Your Habits To Create Your Position of Power*. Tiffany is also the co-founder of three businesses: Anointed Urban Development LLC., Holy Anointed Ministries International, and The Agape Network. Tiffany is the visionary and CEO of Mandatory Success Visions where she serves ministers, healers, holistic practitioners, luminaries, artists, and others who want to transmit a message of love to make impact in the world. She is effective in her business by teaching others how to implement their visions and impact the masses. Beginning in 2015, Tiffany will be offering personal coaching, business coaching, and memberships to insider-only information for business and personal transformation.

## REACH YOUR HIGHEST POTENTIAL!

Tiffany will also be hosting workshops alongside her Mandatory Success business partners where she will be teaching others to effectively embrace their visions, monetize their gifts and talents, and reach the masses.

Tiffany Domena has 20 years experience in the arts with literary art and visual art as her primary areas of expertise. She is also a gifted worship songstress and dancer. Tiffany has 10+ years experience in ministry, leadership, and Real Estate. She has served 9 years in the Air Force Active Duty specializing in Preventative Medicine. Tiffany ensured 4K+ Airmen were deployable; she has inspected hundreds of facilities for sanitation, performed expert tasks in Entomology, supervised many, and assisted with providing thousands of personnel preventative measures to ensure their health. Tiffany holds her BS in Religion from Liberty University, and presently she is continuing her education with the goal of completing her Master's of Divinity in Evangelism and Church Planting thru Liberty University.

Tiffany Domena is assured to be your expert in the areas of:
 -Marriage
-Conflict Resolution
-Real Estate

**THE WORLD NEEDS THE GIFT THAT ONLY YOU HAS!**

-Purpose-driven Life
-Connecting To God
-Relationships
-Business
-Art
-Book Writing
-Book Publishing
-Digital Product Creation
-Marketing
-Publicity
-Maximizing Your Life Potential
-And Many More Areas not yet listed…

To Contact Tiffany Domena for interviews, to book speaking engagements, or for further information, please visit http://www.mandatorysuccess.com/stephen-and-tiffany-domena/.

**REACH YOUR HIGHEST POTENTIAL!**

# OTHER BOOKS BY THIS AUTHOR

### I WANT TO GET MY CHRISTIAN LIFE TOGETHER, BUT WHERE DO I START?

DESCRIPTION:
Everyone needs a foundation; without it, one will fall. This book seeks to help you to build your Christian foundation, so that you can be successful in everything that you pursue in life. If your desire is to understand Christ or to be a better follower, check this book out.

### I WANT TO HAVE IMPACT, BUT WHO SHOULD BE MY MENTOR?

DESCRIPTION:
Do you want to have impact in your life? A life of stagnancy is not fulfilling, and does not bring joy. Our purpose is to serve others, but who can lead you in that? Who can give you ideas about how to have the greatest impact? This book is about the person that had the most impact in all history. Can you guess who this person is? Check this book out and see. ORDER YOUR COPY TODAY!

**THE WORLD NEEDS THE GIFT THAT ONLY YOU HAS!**

## SOMEONE COVETS YOU:

## AN ALLEGORY THAT EXPOSES THE SUBLIMINAL BATTLES OF OUR LIVES

DESCRIPTION:

Have you faced opposition? Do you know your greatest opponent? This book impersonates your invisible opponents so that you can get an understanding of how they still theprominence in your life. If you need liberation and freedom from opposition, get the wisdom from this text.

**REACH YOUR HIGHEST POTENTIAL!**

# OTHER PRODUCTS BY THE AUTHOR

**REACHING OUR HIGHEST POTENTIAL WITH STEPHEN AND TIFFANY DOMENA (ON ITUNES AND STITCHER)**

**THE WORLD NEEDS THE GIFT THAT ONLY YOU HAS!**

# Work With Us On Personal Transformation

## What is the Mandatory Success Personal Transformation Membership?

Perception personal transformation is a development from the book, Perception: The World's Most Affluent Leader.

*Perception Personal Transformation* also includes interactive components like monthly Q&A teleseminars where the founders answer questions and offer strategic advice to ensure that our members take consistent action and receive the highest value from their investment.

Plus, we will always over-deliver! You can stay as long as you would like, however, you will grow to love our community, and we would love to keep you! We want you to be wherever you will get the maximum gain for your success, so if at anytime, you need to cancel, you can do so with no questions asked (we would love to hear your feedback, though).

## Who Should join Perception Personal Transformation?

The ideal person for the perception package includes:

-Ambitious people who want to make loads of impact

-Individuals who need to reshape the environment

**REACH YOUR HIGHEST POTENTIAL!**

with goal-oriented people

-People who need direction to reshape their outlook on their lives and get focused on their purpose.

If this is you, allow Mandatory Success to be a new community for you. Let us surround you with like-minded people, encourage you monthly, and hold you accountable to your success!

### What's included in Perception Personal Transformation?

Are you trying to make impact in your life, but finding a hard time finding accountability and direction? Transformation is not easy when your environment is not fitting and you are not encircled with like-minded people. Become a part of Stephen and Tiffany Domena's Mandatory Success Community. Monthly, you will receive:

-Access to our *Perception Personal Transformation* members-only content

-Weekly Personal Transformation newsletter via email

-Monthly Q&A teleseminars with Stephen and Tiffany Domena where we offer personal transformation advice and answers to your questions.

-Monthly video posts

-Monthly goal setting and time management reminders

-Access to our private member only forums!

-Extra goodies because we ALWAYS over-deliver!

**THE WORLD NEEDS THE GIFT THAT ONLY YOU HAS!**

Who Should join Perception Personal Transformation?

The ideal person for the perception package includes:

-Ambitious people who want to make loads of impact

-Individuals who need to reshape the environment with goal-oriented people

-People who need direction to reshape their outlook on their lives and get focused on their purpose.

If this is you, allow Mandatory Success to be a new community for you. Let us surround you with like-minded people, encourage you monthly, and hold you accountable to your success!

 -Access to our private member only forums!

## What topics will be discussed?

-Life Purpose
-Purpose-driven thought
-Personal Value
-Time Management
-Priorities
-Mentorship
-Overcoming Obstacles
-Identifying blessing time
-Choosing a purpose-embracing environment
-Connecting With God

**REACH YOUR HIGHEST POTENTIAL!**

-Being led to purpose by God

For a low monthly price:
REGULARLY
NOW ONLY $180.00 ANNUALLY -OR- $50.00 for the first month; $15.00/monthly!

Still undecided? Stop by our site and take a quick survey to see if this membership and community would meet your needs.

**THE WORLD NEEDS THE GIFT THAT ONLY YOU HAS!**

# Transformational Personal Coaching

## A Mind-Shifting Personal Coaching Program

Connect to Purpose, Power, and Love
Liberate yourself from past limitations and habits
Stay inspired and motivated to experience MORE of your greatness
Connect to your purpose, value, love, and power
Realize the potential of your life or business
Price: $1800.00
Schedule Your 9 Sessions Over 12 Weeks!

Are you ready to experience MORE of your greatness? It's time for YOU to get out of your own way and BE the breakthrough you've been waiting for. Imagine what life could be like when you wake up every day feeling inspired and motivated to achieve everything you've always wanted. We will help liberate you from hinderances and get UNSTUCK, so you can awaken to your deepest desires and live your greatest dreams.

## Overview of the Topics:

**REACH YOUR HIGHEST POTENTIAL!**

Our Personal Coaching Program teaches you the skills you will need to start living a purpose driven life!
What is included in the Personal Coaching:

Lesson 1:   Introduction
Traits of purpose drive life, traits of how purpose driven life is attained
Lesson 2:   Grasping Your Purpose
Identifying the connection between your obligation and your life purpose; ensuring that your life is supportive of your purpose
Lesson 3:   Free Your areas of mastery
Ensuring that you maximize your areas of mastery within your life
Lesson 4:   Identifying When You Are Out Of Place
Identifying the signs of incorrect placement
Lesson 5:   Personal Time Management
Establishing time priorities and schedules
Lesson 6:   Becoming Universe-Conscious
Learning the impact of universal position and seasons on circumstance
Lesson 7:   Personal Goals
How to create goals that lead to success
Lesson 8:   Know How To Connect To Your Source
How dreams, visions, the audible voice, the angels, and the Holy
Spirit can guide you to greater fulfillment

**THE WORLD NEEDS THE GIFT THAT ONLY YOU HAS!**

Lesson 9: Wrap-up
Summarize everything and answer final questions
You'll spend 12 weeks focused on the most important person in your life… YOU!

You don't have to be held back by past challenges or pain anymore. By motivating yourself, you'll be able to inspire everyone around you and live a life of greatness that transforms both you and those you love. What's your greatest vision? Let's achieve it, together!

For more products or information by Tiffany Domena, visit http://www.mandatorysuccess.com.

**REACH YOUR HIGHEST POTENTIAL!**

# ONE LAST THING...

If you enjoyed this book or found it useful I'd be very grateful if you'd post a short review at:

www.mandatorysuccess.com

While you are there, you can use the coupon code **TRANSFORMATION4ME** for a FREE download of the audiobook. When you visit the website and get on my email list, I will be sure to notify you first about when the Perception Personal Transformation Membership Program will be open. I would love to interact with you via the live Q&As, the live forums, and by seeing your responses to my newsletters. Your support really does make a difference and I read all the reviews personally so I can get your feedback and make this book even better.

Tiffany Domena